Ex Libris

Y0-CDJ-480

"Drake Island is not for career girls!"

Greg's powerful arms grasped Kate's as he went on, "A woman has to be a warm, loving homemaker...and you're not that, are you, Kate?"

She tried to break away. "I never said I was." How could she deal with this sun-bronzed giant whose curly-lashed eyes and joking manner disguised a hard and vengeful character?

"No, you didn't," he snapped, apparently enjoying her struggles. "So what does that make you, hmm? The other sort, the provocative, persuasive type of woman?"

"I think you better leave," Kate stated, fear running an icy finger down her back.

But Greg's only response was to pull her closer and murmur, "I think not, my little temptress...."

Harlequin Premiere Editions

Harlequin
Premiere
Editions

THE
LION'S DEN
Ann Cooper

Harlequin Books

TORONTO · LONDON · LOS ANGELES · AMSTERDAM
SYDNEY · HAMBURG · PARIS · STOCKHOLM · ATHENS · TOKYO

Original hardcover edition published in 1979
by Mills & Boon Limited

ISBN 0-373-82102-6

This Harlequin Premiere Editions volume
published October 1981

Copyright© 1979 by Ann Cooper.
Philippine copyright 1979. Australian copyright 1979.
All rights reserved. Except for use in any review, the reproduction or
utilization of this work in whole or in part in any form by any electronic,
mechanical or other means, now known or hereafter invented, including
xerography, photocopying and recording, or in any information storage or
retrieval system, is forbidden without the permission of the publisher,
Harlequin Enterprises Limited, 225 Duncan Mill Road, Don Mills, Ontario,
Canada M3B 3K9. All the characters in this book have no existence outside
the imagination of the author and have no relation whatsoever to anyone
bearing the same name or names. They are not even distantly inspired by
any individual known or unknown to the author, and all the incidents are
pure invention.

The Harlequin trademark, consisting of the words HARLEQUIN PREMIERE
EDITIONS and the portrayal of a Harlequin, is registered in the United
States Patent Office and in the Canada Trade Marks Office.

Printed in U.S.A.

THE
LION'S DEN

CHAPTER ONE

Now Kate knew why there were never many visitors to Drake Island. People only came with a purpose, she had been told, and battling her way towards the shelter of a low airport building, she wondered if *her* purpose had a hope of remaining a secret for very long.

It was a bright November morning; it was supposed to be early summer, although Kate found it as cold as the wintry weather she had left behind in England. A vicious wind blew her long, dark hair in all directions, and she knew the icy gusts had travelled hundreds of miles over the treacherous waters of the South Atlantic Ocean. Cape Horn, Tierra del Fuego and beyond—Antarctica. These had been names to conjure with, especially from the comfort of International Petroleum's London office. But all her colleagues in Inpet were over eight thousand miles away. If she was supposed to be on a photographic mission it would be as well to forget them. From now on Kate was definitely alone.

'You enjoyed the flight, Miss Lawrence?' asked the

ground hostess who had come out to meet them. She wasn't clairvoyant; Kate had been the only woman passenger on the plane from Chile, and as they halted for a small private aircraft to taxi in front of them, Kate thought the young girl could probably put a name to the other four passengers as well. Two of the men were Government officials relieving colleagues at the Meteorological Station, another was a young shepherd beginning a four-year contract on one of the outlying settlements, and the fourth man worked for the same company as Kate. He was an oil man who had come to settle some crisis on a rig. That was the problem with offshore rigs, Kate frowned inwardly, they were always more time and more trouble. Naturally the man didn't realise she was also on the Inpet payroll. Only one man on Drake Island knew the real reason for Kate's visit, and he would keep well out of the way.

The straggly group began its battle towards shelter again as the little red and white single-engine plane swung away from them and came to an abrupt halt in front of the airport building. The stewardess told their co-pilot—who had accompanied them across the tarmac—that the Cherokee had brought the final three passengers for his flight back to the mainland. That all the passengers had been able to assemble in good time appeared to be a matter for some comment. But Kate, who couldn't see the wonder in it, found herself thinking instead that the conditions were far too windy for such a tiny aircraft. Therefore it was a relief when she was finally shepherded into the warm building.

Kate felt like the spy who came in from the cold, then guiltily changed her mind. Not spy, that was coming it too strong. Mata Hari, perhaps? Yes, that sounded more flamboyant, and much to her surprise the police officer doing his immigration stint allowed Kate Lawrence, alias Mata Hari, into Her Majesty's Colony of Drake Island.

The procedure for five passengers didn't take long, but when their cases arrived Kate realised she'd left her gadget-bag full of cameras on the plane.

Nobody seemed to mind the inconvenience, and as the First Officer had to return to the plane, he was happy to accompany Kate.

It only took a minute to collect the bag from beneath her seat, and the young fellow was still busy in the cockpit when Kate was ready to leave. 'I'll make my own way back,' she called out, and he nodded a brief smile from his seat, mathematical calculations obviously spinning round in his head.

Once a day ought to be sufficient for this sort of trek, Kate thought, as the wind began cruelly whipping at her hair again. The plane had been 'parked', if that was the right word, in a convenient place for unloading cargo. Understandably, five passengers hardly constituted VIP treatment, and leaning into the wind again, she began the long and difficult walk back to the tiny Customs Hall.

Kate wasn't really looking where she was going,

but then this wasn't Heathrow, aircraft weren't exactly thick on the ground. Suddenly the young pilot began revving the twin engines and perhaps that was why Kate didn't hear the approaching plane as it taxied towards her. Only at the last moment she heard a noise, and swivelled round in alarm. The little plane lurched to a halt again, the pilot seemed to be making a habit of it, and he scowled at her long and hard, or Kate suspected he did, for with dark glasses and headset it was difficult to read his expression. But she had no such problem a few minutes later when she was finally clearing her luggage through the almost deserted Customs Hall.

The door from an adjoining office burst open and Kate had no doubt that this was the heavy-handed—or was it heavy-footed?—pilot. The door banged shut behind him, it was a wonder the glass didn't break, and he began unbuttoning his thick leather jacket as he strode towards her. Kate was used to meeting antagonism head on, but as his dark, vibrant eyes tore into her she felt strangely breathless. He had the strong, powerful look of a man used to fighting the elements—and used to winning.

'And just *what* do you think you were doing out there? You could have been killed!' he roared, practically flinging his clipboard on to the counter next to her cases. He had a rich, dark brown voice that oozed authority. It did odd things to Kate's nervous system, but not enough to throw her completely off balance. He needn't think *I'm* jumping to attention, she thought hotly, as his next words made the Customs officer shuffle. 'Who let you out there? Why were you wandering around? This isn't exactly a pleasure garden, you know!'

Kate pulled herself upright. She would have liked to stare him straight in the eye, but she didn't have a step-ladder; of course he just had to be a six-foot giant. What had happened to all those nice five-foot weaklings? His thick, dark chestnut hair was disarrayed giving him a wild, almost savage look, and as his eyes continued their hostility she wished he'd kept on his sunglasses.

'I don't know why you kept coming towards me, for that matter,' Kate argued, putting on her best hoity-toity voice. 'Couldn't you have blown your horn or something?' she added stupidly, and his anger turned quickly to utter disbelief.

'I pilot aeroplanes, madam, not Noddy cars,' was the clipped reply, and with a nod of recognition at last to the man beside her, he picked up his clipboard and hurtled back through the door the way he'd come. He shouldn't have been flying planes, thought Kate, who was still smarting at the title *madam*. He'd have looked more at home on an Elizabethan galleon—a pirate sailing the Southern Ocean for a sight of land.

'Not exactly the warmest of welcomes,' Kate said frostily as she picked up her bags.

'Gets in a rare old temper at times, does Mr Henderson,' the Customs man admitted, 'but don't you worry about him, miss, soon blows over, it does,' and he helped Kate to carry her bags through to the Arrivals lounge.

'Did you say *Henderson*?' Kate pulled up quickly when the name had sunk in.

'That's right, Greg Henderson. Owns Sealbank Settlement and runs the Inter-Island Airways. Quite a well-known character hereabouts,' he added, and Kate knew in that respect he wasn't totally correct. Greg Henderson's notoriety spread further afield than Drake Island. His name was often bandied about in London, it headed the dossier in her case, and it was all because of Greg Henderson that she'd travelled eight thousand miles to this minuscule speck in the Southern Hemisphere.

'But at least I've made contact,' she muttered to herself when she was finally alone, although it was probably not the kind of contact her employer had had in mind when he had suggested this assignment. They had been in the comfortable, centrally-heated, fifteenth-floor office, overlooking Hyde Park.

'Okay!' Kate had admitted at last. 'So I did a good P.R. job up in Scotland, but what makes you think I can handle this fellow?' She had tapped the file on her lap. 'He sounds a bit of a handful.' And her boss, 'Big John' the men called him, had peered over his half-frame spectacles.

'Katherine,' he began, clearing his throat. That was a bad sign. He only called her Katherine under pressure and she realised her case was practically lost.

'Katherine,' he repeated, 'didn't you think those Highland villagers were a handful? I would have thought that was putting it mildly. But you've got a silken tongue, my girl, when it suits you—and if you can persuade them that the coming of oil is beneficial, then this Henderson fellow will be a walk-over!'

'But what about Dougal McInnes?' Kate wasn't giving up without a fight. 'If he's running the base down there for the offshore rigs, then surely he's just the person to do the persuading, and *he's* on hand.'

Big John dropped his gaze to the leatherbound blotting pad. 'Ah, well, there's a wee problem with our Dougal,' he said, mimicking the Scotsman.

'You mean Dougal doesn't get on with him, either?'

'Let me be straight with you.' He looked seriously at Kate. 'We've tried every method we know to get Greg Henderson's permission to drill on his land. We've written time and time again, but apart from that one letter he doesn't reply. Dougal's been to see him, but he gets practically thrown off the settlement. Why to heaven Henderson won't let us out there, I can't imagine.'

'And if we can't drill at Sealbank it means another offshore rig?' Kate said, wanting to get the point quite straight.

'Exactly! Mind you, we don't know yet that the tests will be conclusive. But you can imagine the seas out there, Kate. It's bad enough having the offshore rigs on the other side of the Island. But that latest report,' he pointed to the folder on Kate's lap, 'could be a big one, but it's right down south, away from the other rigs and in even worse seas. If we can get on that southerly promontory it's got to be good news.'

'And you think *I* can persuade him.' Kate flicked open the folder and ran her eyes over the first page. 'He's thirty-five,' she read, 'a bachelor, and you think a man like that—living down there—is going to take one scrap of notice of anything I have to say. He's a good ten years older than me. He'll think I'm a child ...' she broke off. Big John was eyeing her speculatively.

'I don't think the man will look upon you as a child,' he said wickedly, his gaze running over her neat figure. 'Maybe he is cut off down there—a bit of a chauvinist, even. Isn't that what you girls call a fellow with a bit of spirit, these days?' Kate decided not to take that subject further and Big John went on: 'So if he's a red-blooded male, Kate, and lonely, perhaps you'll be just what he needs.'

Kate laughed to herself, remembering Big John's words, as she crossed the Arrivals lounge and went out into the wind again. She might be many things to many people, she realised, her good humour returning, but Greg Henderson probably needed her like he needed a sore head.

Apart from a small gathering of passengers for the weekly flight out, the airport had a forlorn atmosphere. Kate received a few smiles, but no one offered to help with her cases. That was the problem, she realised, of appearing to be independent. Even Big

John thought she could dash around the world pouring some of his oil on troubled waters. No one ever tried to smooth a calm way for Kate. Perhaps she should have engineered a little-girl-lost appearance, it would certainly have come in handy just now. Kate groaned inwardly. Imagine making such an awful beginning to the operation! Even if Greg Henderson was overbearing and egotistical, she should have played her part with more professionalism.

Now that she was outside Kate looked around with interest, having had only a brief glimpse of the scenery from the plane's window before landing. There had been a wild, rugged shore, a distant mountain range and bleak, featureless landscape with no apparent habitation. Then the aircraft had banked before lining up with the runway and there had been the sight of Francistown, the Island's tiny city, where she had seen brightly coloured houses clinging to the hills around the natural harbour. Then they had touched down a few seconds later, although now, Kate realised, they were probably several miles from civilisation and there didn't appear to be any taxis about either. In fact, there was nothing beyond the airport's few low buildings but mile upon mile of harsh, rocky landscape with a few tracks disappearing through the bracken and boulders. There wasn't a tree anywhere, and if the sun hadn't been shining, Kate guessed, the prospect would have appeared extremely gloomy. Even the air smelt different, although perhaps 'smelt' was a contradiction in terms, for it carried no lingering hint of the land, and when she breathed deeply Kate was aware of the vast Antarctic continent over which the wind had passed. It had a fresh, pure quality she could almost taste. It made her feel very wide-awake, which was perhaps just as well, because it looked as if she would have to carry her bags all the way to the hotel.

A door banged further along the building, and Kate glanced round automatically, hoping it was someone whose help she could enlist. But she very soon changed her mind when she saw the towering figure of Greg Henderson. Unsure of the sensation the sight of him had caused, Kate turned away quickly, and tried to look as if she was waiting for someone special. She wasn't going to ask Greg Henderson anything, but then it appeared she didn't have to. He jumped into a Land Rover and roared off, only to screech to a halt a few feet away from her.

'I will *not* ask him for a lift,' thought Kate firmly. 'I don't care if I've ten miles to walk.' But before she realised what was happening, Greg Henderson had picked up her two suitcases and had practically thrown them into the rear of his vehicle.

'And just what do you think you're doing?' Kate demanded angrily. 'I'm—I'm just waiting for my lift.'

'I'm your lift,' he informed her coolly, and she could tell he was making a big effort to keep calm.

'I didn't arrange for you——' Kate began, and broke off as the wretched man climbed back into his seat.

'If you're coming I suggest you get in,' he called through the passenger window, and as Kate was pretty sure he would have gone without her she scrambled up beside him.

'I could have waited for a taxi,' she said ungraciously, aware of an odd prickly irritableness, making it important that she shouldn't look at him.

'You'd have waited a long time.' He manoeuvred the Land Rover around crates of freight before continuing: 'We don't happen to have any taxis on Drake—the inhabitants don't need any.'

'But what about visitors?' asked Kate, turning at last to glance at his stern profile.

'We don't have that many visitors.' The Land Rover leapt forward. 'And those we do are usually met by friends or colleagues.' He seemed to be suggesting that without either of these she was in some way deficient.

'And what about the rest?—like me,' said Kate. 'You're surely not saying outsiders never come here. I would have thought you'd have had more faith in your island, Mr Henderson.'

'Most—*photographers*—come with the Antarctic team.' There was a veiled hint of scepticism in his tone.

'How do you know I'm a photographer?' she blurted, then was cross with herself for sounding worried.

'Everyone knows everything about strangers on Drake,' he said, almost conversationally, although

Kate couldn't see how this was possible so soon after her arrival.

She fell silent, trying to work out her position and surreptitiously watching him from the corner of her eye. He seemed an odd mixture. He had the rugged outdoor appearance of the farmer, which matched the vehicle in which they were travelling. Yet his large, square hands on the steering wheel were well-kept and his immaculate slacks and blue lambswool sweater had the elegant timeless look of quality that went with his pilot's image. And where would the oil tycoon fit in? Kate wondered. If Inpet did discover an economic amount of oil at Sealbank, Greg Henderson would be a very rich man indeed. But then he must realise that, Kate thought impatiently. So why wasn't he giving them a chance to make his fortune? She stole another glance at the strong, capable face and powerful, packed-with-dynamite frame of the man beside her. He would be a good person to have on your side in a fight, she realised. But she certainly didn't fancy him as the opponent he undoubtedly was.

They didn't pass any other traffic on the way to town, and Kate, finding the growing atmosphere in the cab unsettling, decided to try and concentrate on the scenery.

In a terrifying way it was magnificent, with the bleak, rough ground scarred by peat-cutting. Yet the picture was somehow softened by the distant mauve haze of the mountain ridge she had seen from the air. In between the boulders and bracken were patches of brilliant green, sprinkled with masses of tiny, bright flowers. These were bogs, Greg informed her, when she had commented, and suddenly they hadn't looked quite so pretty after all.

Gradually the broad plain was giving way to gently rising hills, the sea shimmered away to the right, and the truck slowed down to climb the winding road as it neared the town.

At the top of the hill Greg pulled to a halt and there, tumbling below them, were the clusters of brightly coloured houses and neat harbour she had seen from the air. Only it wasn't the houses—which were mostly white timber—but the roofs, that were reflecting reds, greens and blues with the help of the sun. Even the sea seemed to be putting on a special show; it was green—a deep, deep green—and beyond the shelter of the headland the tops of the waves were peeling off in foamy white horses, as spectacular as any equestrian event.

'I didn't imagine it would be like this,' whispered Kate, who had been expecting the starkness of a science-fiction moonbase.

Greg Henderson seemed pleased. Could there be a touch of pride, even? Kate wondered, glancing at him quickly as he slipped into gear and rolled downhill. For a second his hard, almost suspicious look had slipped away, but now the shutters were back down and she found herself staring instead at his large, square cut hands negotiating the Land Rover around hairpin bends.

Before the final steep descent to the harbour he turned off towards a headland upon which was perched an hotel. He came to a stop beside a drystone wall and it was only when all the gear had been unloaded that Kate realised she hadn't told him in which hotel she was staying.

'There *is* only one hotel,' he announced airily, the wind whipping his hair haywire as it gusted across the promontory. Kate was having the same trouble and decided this wasn't the time to put Greg Henderson in his place. But the time wouldn't be very long in the coming, she decided, following him around to the front of the two-storey building.

The hotel was a surprise, as the picturesque view of the town had been. It was a family business, Kate knew, and she hadn't been prepared for the modern taste of luxury. The deep red carpets and curtains, the large double-glazed windows, central heating, and the gentle sound of music drifting out from the lounge.

Her amazement must have shown, because Greg Henderson looked down from his lofty height and seemed all too ready to disillusion her.

'Don't be misled by the opulence,' he said, his tone making Kate's hackles rise. 'This is just for the tourists, along with the plastic penguins.' Then dropping his voice menacingly, he added: 'You'll have to go much further afield to achieve what you've come for!'

What did he mean by that? Did he really know, or had he just been talking about the photographs? Kate couldn't decide, and there wasn't time to speculate as she signed in and was shown to her room.

But Kate unpacked automatically, nervously flicking her hair into place, as she gradually began to realise the awkwardness of her position. She hadn't intended spinning Greg Henderson such a yarn. But then she hadn't been prepared to bump into him so soon after touch-down. She knew from reports sent to London that Drake Island was a pretty tight community and the idea of being a photographer had been to gain access, and maybe a few days' grace, in which time she would have arranged to see Henderson and calmly and tactfully explain her purpose in coming. Yet it was almost as if he had been expecting her. And her response to his challenge had been automatic. Kate cursed herself for not having had more control. Now it was going to be difficult to retract. And as jeans followed dresses into the wardrobe she wondered how such a fierce man would react when she did finally manage to tell him the truth.

Kate didn't mind dining alone that evening at the end of such a tiring day, and gradually she unwound while the sky streaked from pearly pink to deepest mauve, as night closed in over the sea. The lights around the harbour, down in Francistown, winked up at her. Yet such cosiness was an illusion, she knew. Only strong double-glazing protected her from the buffeting gale outside. If Greg Henderson had flown out to his farm tonight, he would have had a very uncomfortable journey.

But when coffee was served in the lounge, Kate pushed away all fears for a dominant sheep farmer as the one or two other guests included her in their fireside conversation.

It had been a long day, and a little after ten-thirty Kate said goodnight and made her way out of the lounge towards the stairs. She had noticed earlier that the front door was kept closed against the wind, but now it was opened and someone came in when Kate had climbed only a couple of steps. The cold draught brought with it a wild restlessness that she couldn't define, but she knew the peace of the evening had vanished.

Footsteps crossed the tiled hall; heavy footsteps, well spaced out footsteps, like those belonging to a very big man.

Kate could feel her back tingle, as if someone was watching her, and she had to resist a powerful temptation to turn round and see who it was. The footsteps reached the stairs and ascended them lightly, athletically, probably two at a time, and Kate felt the involuntary quickening of her own pace. She turned left at the landing—so did he. Because it was a *he*, and he was getting closer. An unreasonable fear prickled her scalp. Look round, she told herself. It could be anyone ... But she knew it wasn't, and to look round would prove something. What exactly, she wasn't sure.

Any moment Kate expected to feel his hand reach out and touch her, he was getting nearer and her heart thudded as she fished for her key. Two more doors—one—then she was turning towards her own, holding out the key with trembling fingers, but it was too late. Greg Henderson had stopped right behind her, and one glance backwards told her all she needed to know. Faint mockery twisted his lips. He could have caught up with her back on the stairs, or spoken —anything. But he hadn't, and he'd been perfectly aware of his cat and mouse tactics. The swine!

Now he leant against the door post, one hand on the frame above their heads, his solid bulk totally blocking any means of escape. He was wearing a pale green shirt, woollen tie and a tweedy jacket the colour of bracken. Close-fitting trousers covered long, powerful legs and a well-shod foot protruded in front of her.

'Settling in?' he asked casually, the cleft in his chin deepening.

'Several hours ago,' Kate pointed out stiffly, at the same time wondering how she was going to get into her room and keep him out of it. 'But thank you for being concerned,' she added firmly, willing him to go, but it was useless. He just stood there, all tough bronzed male, watching her shrewdly.

'Lonely?' His curly lashes flickered as he surveyed her from top to toe. But the action was automatic, his eyes were all cold hardness. He was playing a part, and he continued it by adding: 'Aren't you going to invite me in?'

The nerve of the man! 'I don't know quite what type of woman you've been used to down here,' Kate began, without thinking of her vulnerability, 'but I'm from the civilised world, and there we act with a little more decorum!'

His eyes flashed, but his expression remained a mask, and he just shrugged. 'That's your problem, honey. But you're on Drake now, and you know what they say—when in Rome . . .'

'Not in this case,' she interrupted quickly, and the corners of his mouth drooped.

'Still, if you change your mind I'm only in the room next door.' His eyes lingered suggestively. 'You're quite sure . . .?'

'Perfectly! Now, if you don't mind, Mr Henderson . . .' It was the second time she had called him by name, but now he chose to question it as one eyebrow arched. 'The Customs officer told me.' Which was true, wasn't it? 'He seemed quite used to apologising for your behaviour,' she continued arrogantly, 'although I suppose it's the least I can expect from . . .'

'From people like us?' Greg finished for her, his brow creasing with anger. 'But didn't they tell you what to expect, back in London?' Her eyes flew to his face, but before she realised what was happening Greg caught hold of both her wrists and pulled her violently against him.

Her small cry was stifled as her face pounded into his massive chest, and her nose tingled with the smell of tweed and aftershave. 'Let me *go*!' She wriggled uselessly, and the hands that controlled her flying fists suddenly tightened, the solid mass of body went rigid, and he pinned her arms behind her back with a force that was almost terrifying. Then he snatched the key from her grasp, unlocked the door and hauled her unceremoniously into the darkened room. He groped for one of the light switches and, by chance, hit the one that lit only a soft light over her bed.

'You shouldn't have come, Kate. Not down here—among us savages—because you never know what might happen.'

'I didn't say—you're exaggerating—get out of my room *now*!' Kate's eyes glared dangerously, but he wasn't impressed.

'No way, honey!' He pulled her even tighter against him and Kate gasped at the shattering intimacy of his long, hard body. 'You see what you do to me!' His eyes ravaged her. 'Mind you, you're a bit young for my taste, but I expect what you lack in experience you'll make up for with enthusiasm. I'll admit I've seen far worse flown in!'

Kate tried to control the rise and fall of her chest, for that, she guessed, would make him gloat all the more. 'You're not suggesting . . .'

'I never suggest, I'm telling you, but it'll probably be better for waiting.' His lips twisted and she saw the devil come into his eyes. 'But we can always try this just for openers.' And before she could even think of stopping him, his sensuous mouth cruelly covered hers, and savage hands attacked with little regard for her feelings. Kate struggled and protested, but the total effect was dynamite. 'What else did you expect from a man down here?' Greg growled eventually, surveying the result of his aggressive work-out. 'Like I said, honey, we're not civilised—so you'd better be prepared for anything!'

For ten seconds Kate was rooted to the spot as they stared at each other in fury. Then he left, and she slammed the door, locked it and marched over to the bed.

Hadn't Big John warned her that Greg Henderson might be a wild chauvinist suffering from the effects of a restricted love-life? What had John said? Kate racked her brain. There were four men to every one woman on Drake. And of those four hundred or so females only twenty-five per cent were over the age of consent or under fifty, and that wasn't discounting the happily married women. Statistics like those certainly narrowed the field for men like Greg Henderson, and she guessed he fitted extremely well into John's explicit sketch of life on the Island. Kate threw her bag on to the bed and began marching about. Greg Henderson was nothing but a ruthless, uncivilised brute, yet he needn't think he could snap her up for a few moments' pleasure. This might be the South Atlantic Ocean, but that had been a Union Jack she had seen flying from a building. The same rules applied down here. Although later, as she turned off the bedside lamp and snuggled down to sleep, Kate doubted that Greg Henderson had heard of many rules; and those he had he had probably broken, time and time again.

CHAPTER TWO

TONIGHT Kate found sleep would not come easily. Her heart continued its violent throbbing and she tossed and turned in the darkened room, wide awake and seething.

It was all *his* fault. She stretched out her hand and touched the wall that separated this room from Greg's. Was he really there, maybe in bed only a few inches away? Her hand recoiled, as if the wall had been made of glass and he was behind it, inspecting every move she made. The man was a menace! Kate wriggled in the bed and tried to dispel his image, but she couldn't, his face swam before her defiantly.

And this was the man with whom Big John expected her to negotiate? This sunbronzed giant with the wide-awake face and a devilish cleft in his chin. Yet curly lashes and gentle propositions were deceptive. Already Kate had discovered they were little more than a disguise, kept in place to fool the unwary. How easily the eyes flew open, glinting dangerously. And how easily the face hardened to match the body bent on retribution. She hadn't really said they were

all savages, but how quickly he had pounced on her
one little indiscretion.

Kate could feel those strong hands pulling her
against him and moving intimately over her body
without the slightest reserve. She could feel his cruel
mouth, trapping hers, and the exquisite agony of her
own trembling arousal.

'But you were tired,' Kate told herself sharply,
'caught off guard, not expecting such an onslaught
even from Greg Henderson.' But worst of all was wondering if he had recognised her response. And would
his punishment be to repeat it? Or to choose not to?

Morning was never one of Kate's best times, and
after a restless night the woolly ball of confusion sat
between her eyes more heavily than usual. Early
morning tea hadn't dispelled it and now, at breakfast, she was reaching for the coffee pot with a certain desperation.

Today was Tuesday, and it was going to have to
be 'be-nice-to-Greg-Henderson-day'. Maybe someone
should sell flags, thought Kate, chuckling to herself.
He probably wasn't that bad. He was rough—not
used to women—and his aggressive behaviour probably hid his basic insecurity. Kate was beginning to
believe her comfortable theory. If I'm pleasant to him
surely it won't be so hard to win his confidence. And
after a few days, maybe I can bring the subject round
to oil ... She paused in her thoughts and added
cream to her coffee. Or maybe it would be best to give
it to him straight. Go out and see him at the airport.

Or better still, go out to Sealbank. Give him the facts,
explain the benefits. But wouldn't that be taking a
risk? Like walking straight into the lions' den. But
with Kate's sort of job she had to take risks, play the
game by instinct rather than by the book. But her
instincts regarding Greg Henderson were not of the
type that bore close inspection, and as he strolled into
the dining room at that precise moment Kate felt
curiously edgy and flustered as he approached.

He was carrying a pile of books, and she tried not
to notice the easy confidence with which he weaved
his way between empty tables, bringing into such
comfortable, safe surroundings the restlessness of
outdoors.

Never mind if you'd like to knock him into the
middle of next week, she told herself sharply. You're
here to do a job, my girl, and the sooner it's done the
sooner you can leave the blessed man behind you.

'And how's our intrepid photographer this morning?' he asked eventually, stopping at her table and
gazing down with inscrutable dark eyes at her up-
turned face. The enemy was never so bad when finally
faced, Kate realised, and with only the slightest
qualm she gave him a beautiful good-morning smile.
He pulled out the chair she indicated with a gesture,
and tucked the books out of the way by his feet. Suddenly he was sitting opposite, smiling warmly. It was
as if her mind had conjured him by magic. Or had he
conjured himself by magic? Kate shivered.

'Do you mind?' he asked, picking up the coffee pot

and judging its contents, and when Kate agreed, he helped himself, glancing momentarily at her face as he waited for the cup to fill.

'Cream, sugar?' she enquired. This was ridiculous, it wasn't really happening, not after their blazing row last night. But it was, and Kate watched him stir a trail of whiteness into his dark drink. She caught him watching her again, and when their eyes met he held hers, but the smile on his lips didn't extend beyond them.

'I don't usually breakfast in such charming company,' came the polished remark, and she wondered if it was to be 'be-nice-to-Kate-day' as well.

Kate accepted the olive branch warily and came back with one of her own. 'I—I think I should apologise for some of the things I said last night.'

'And I'm obviously not used to such sensitive young ladies of sophistication.' The set of his mouth seemed to make a mockery of such words, but his voice had been perfectly even.

'It was late, we were both tired . . .' Kate prevaricated quickly. 'Do you normally stay in the hotel, Mr Henderson? I understand you have a farm . . .'

'Settlement,' he corrected quietly. 'And yes, I normally stay here when the weather grounds me. And that's pretty often, so they keep a room continually at my disposal. It's the easiest arrangement.'

'You must find the Inter-Island Airways keeps you very busy,' Kate continued in her meeting-new-clients voice. 'I believe you started the company

several years ago. You must have a very good manager at your Settlement to run things while you're
away.'

'The airline keeps me very busy. I started it five
years ago. And I have an excellent manager.' He
replaced his cup with a clatter and looked across at
her sardonically. 'Bit early in the day for interviewing, wouldn't you say? Have you a tape-recorder on
your lap? Or just instant recall?'

It took Kate a couple of seconds to fall in. 'Habit,'
she shrugged. 'But I *am* interested, and I'd like to
know more about Sealbank.' If he thought she knew
a lot already he had probably put it down to gossip
in the bar last night.

Just then the waitress came and took his order for
a breakfast of mammoth proportions and when the
woman had gone he sat back in his chair and made no
attempt to hide the fact that he was surveying Kate.
She thought he looked like a man who had done it all
—*seen* it all—and was just wondering in which cate-
gory to put her.

She wriggled uncomfortably under such scrutiny,
and knew somehow she would have to break the
silence. Wasn't she always jumping in with both
feet? Perhaps now was the time to leap in again.

'As you can imagine,' she began carefully, 'coming all this way, with a limited time at my disposal,
I'd like to see as much of the Island as possible . . .'

'Naturally!' came the caustic response, but Kate
wasn't daunted yet.

'I know the economy of the Island depends on sheep farming, so I'd like to visit a settlement, see how things are really run. It would make a good spread,' she added as an afterthought, dangling what she hoped sounded like the front cover of *Time* magazine.

'You've picked a bad time,' Greg countered unhelpfully, laying into a plate of chops that had just arrived.

Kate averted her eyes and pretended it was just toast and marmalade. 'Bad time?' she repeated, attempting to regain his attention.

'We're about to start shearing. All the stations will be rounding up their flocks. That means every available man working full stretch, seven days a week until it's done. Not exactly a good time to go visiting, Miss Lawrence.'

'*Kate*,' she reminded him, successfully softening the harshness of his comment. 'Of course I quite see the problem,' she went on, wondering why she'd never joined the Diplomatic Corps. 'With anyone else it would be quite out of the question.' His fork paused halfway to his mouth and she had the full penetration of those nut-brown eyes, which made continuing calmly almost impossible. 'That—that's why I thought—as you're obviously organised to spend a certain amount of time away from home—you might be able to spare a little of what's left to show me Sealbank. I wouldn't need to take up much of your time once we're there,' she continued hurriedly, when he didn't speak. 'If I could wander round—take plenty of photos—I wouldn't get in the way . . .' It was no good, she was getting more and more breathless, it would be better to shut up altogether.

Greg returned the fork to his plate, dabbed his lips with the check napkin and started looking at her all over again. Only now his eyes lingered on her sleek, dark hair flicking on to her shoulders, on her fine, tapered brows and large, luminous amber eyes. Then he dropped his gaze to her throat and lower, to the enticing curves beneath her soft, turquoise sweater. 'You are nothing—if not—direct,' he said eventually, raising his eyes to meet Kate's. But now there was something else lurking behind his shrewdness. A glimmer of interest? Kate saw the merest hint of the look in his eyes when he had kissed her last night. But then it had been spontaneous, whereas now, it was merely calculated.

Kate nearly choked at his audacity. *He thinks I'm offering to go out there as some sort of—of comfort!* You take me along and I'll make it worth your while. Is that what he's thinking? How big-headed could you get? Were women in that short supply down here? Kate was just about to tell him exactly where he could get off, but she managed to check her ready response. Big John would blush if she said such a thing. And wouldn't she be letting him down—sending her all this way . . . Kate played with a few crumbs on her plate to gain breathing time. If Greg Henderson was as ruthless as this, then she would have to be equally as ruthless. Maybe she could suggest her company might be a benefit. If he chose to take it in any particular way that was his problem. She hadn't yet met a man she couldn't handle if it came to the crunch. 'I think it's much better to be direct,' she began somewhat fatalistically. 'It saves so much time . . .' But he pondered over her remark, not exactly falling over himself with enthusiasm.

'We don't have many visitors at Sealbank,' he said eventually. 'We're beyond the mountains, if the weather closes in you could be stuck there.'

'A few days either way will hardly matter,' Kate murmured, which seemed to amuse him. 'It needn't be all hard work. There could be,' she paused, swallowed, then added: 'compensations!' There, she'd said it, and the response was immediate.

'You civilised young ladies sure have a way with you. It must be very important, this assignment of yours—or do you always mix business with pleasure?'

Cheek! 'Only in special circumstances,' she countered quickly, masking her anger with an impish gleam.

'What makes me so special?' And Kate caught the imperceptible change of tone. 'There are settlements much nearer town. Several, in fact, that you could reach by Land Rover at this time of year.'

'But I know you,' Kate broke in, and now it was her turn to do the roving-eye routine. She forced an expression of pleasure as her eyes lingered over his tousled, dark auburn hair, at his strong face with broad, tanned cheek-bones and firm, cleft chin. She noticed one of his eyebrows quirked at the end, and his eyes were the colour of polished chestnuts. But if she thought to disconcert him by such behaviour, she was sadly mistaken.

'I'm afraid it's out of the question, Miss Lawrence,' he said at last. After such an offer he was turning her down? Kate nearly exploded as he went on: 'You'd be a disrupting influence on my young lads. And I thoroughly disapprove of members of the Press. My sentiments are very well known round here.'

'You're right there, and it's not just the Press you disapprove of, thought Kate quickly. 'I'd like to change your mind,' she managed to say, smiling invitingly.

'I'd like to see you try it!' For a second his eyes flashed and the wry twist left his lips, but its return was immediate. 'But I never change my mind, Miss Lawrence. I find first impressions are usually correct.'

Kate remembered their first meeting and could have cried. 'A gentleman ought to give a lady just one chance . . .' And before he could say he was no gentleman, she continued quickly: 'And I never did thank you for driving me in from the airport. The receptionist told me they usually send out their own transport to meet visitors . . .' She broke off, watching for the slightest hint of suspicion in his reaction. It was one little bit of information that had been bothering her since yesterday evening when she had casually remarked to the young woman behind the desk..

But Greg Henderson didn't seem at all lost for an explanation, and if she didn't know him better, she could have said he looked almost amused. 'You haven't been with us long enough, Miss Lawrence—Kate—to realise that a young woman travelling alone is something of a sensation down here. I'd be a fool if I didn't take advantage of my position.' He spoke slowly, letting the measure of his words fall heavily. 'I saw the passenger list—phoned the hotel,' he shrugged. 'The rest was easy . . .'

For a moment Kate was thunderstruck. Last night, in her bedroom, he had raked his eyes over her and muttered something about seeing far worse flown in. Was that his trick? Did he go round snapping people's names off the passenger list, if he thought it would do him a bit of good? Kate bit the insides of her cheeks and twisted the napkin on her lap into a vicious knot, wishing it was Greg Henderson's throat. The strain of all this would soon send her, screaming, from the room.

'Then wouldn't it be wise to let me come out to Sealbank with you?' she whispered sweetly. 'I mean, if you're that short of women I might be snapped up.'

It didn't look as if the prospect greatly bothered him. 'I shall be back again at the end of the week, maybe I'll give you a ring.'

'It might be too late by then,' Kate suggested, feeling acutely aware of his hard brown eyes surveying her again.

'I doubt it,' he muttered thoughtfully, as if he knew every move she intended to make. Then in the most cold-blooded manner Kate had ever heard, he added: 'It's a pity I'm tied up today. If you're that interested we could have ...' He broke off as if it wasn't necessary for him to say exactly what they could have ...

Kate tried to smile a disappointed sort of smile, but she suddenly had a feeling of intense relief. She had an idea Greg Henderson was not a man to fool with, and for the past ten minutes she'd been playing with fire.

There was no point in hanging about after that, but when she rose to leave, Greg came with her, carrying his pile of books effortlessly under one arm.

'I am expected at the radio station,' he said lightly, when they were out in the reception hall and he was dumping his books on the counter. 'But that's not until eleven—nearly an hour and a half.' His eyes suddenly sparked with a look that turned Kate's knees to water, as he murmured softly. 'And I guess we could do a lot of getting acquainted in that time. What do you say, Kate?' He strolled across to the foot of the stairs and caught hold of her hand. 'We're both adult. Just give me ten minutes and I'll have you eating out of the palm of my hand. Give me twenty minutes and I'll probably be dragging you out to Sealbank and demanding that you stay for a month. Playing it by my rules, of course.' He touched her cheek with the back of his hand. 'But, honey, you'll love them ...'

'Don't kid yourself.' How calmly she stared up at him while his hand lowered and began caressing her throat. She could even meet his eyes casually as if she was always getting propositions from such disturbing monsters. Yet, inside, she was seething with a wild, frantic anger. Oh, how the wretched man infuriated!

Finally she knocked his hand away and he chose to allow it.

'You mean they don't do that kind of thing where you come from?' he taunted.

Kate marched up two steps, lengthening the gap between them, before daring to reply. 'We're not quite so obvious. We get to know people first, form relationships.'

'You don't say!' He leaned against the banister and stared up at her sardonically. 'But that didn't bother you just now. And I'd have thought you hadn't got to know anyone yet, not by the way you get all hot and bothered every time I even touch you.'

Kate could have screamed with frustration. To deny either of his suggestions would put her in the wrong. 'I suppose it's heads you win, tails I lose,' she managed to hiss furiously.

'That's right, honey. Every time. Just you remember it. And don't try starting things you're not equipped to finish. I won't give you a second chance again.'

Mentally tossing him a string of vicious expletives, Kate pounded upstairs as Greg swaggered over to the telephone. 'The Governor's House,' she heard him ask the telephonist, and Kate pulled a face and mimed the same words, shaking her head importantly. Perhaps Greg Henderson was trying to get her deported. That might be the best thing all round.

The wind was still with them today, but when Kate returned to her room and stared out of the window, trying to calm down, she saw that the sun had departed, and an ominous bank of heavy cloud was rumbling in from the West. The sea's deep green had also vanished and had been replaced by a dark, leaden swell that seemed to match the mood of the day. Without the sun, even the houses down in Francistown had lost their brilliance and, to Kate, appeared to be melting into the surrounding, sombre hillsides.

It seemed that everything bowed before the elements—but not Kate. She would put on her bright red mac and paint a splash of colour on to the dismal scene. It seemed suddenly important to prove her immunity.

Fortunately there was no sign of Greg when she came back downstairs, although she saw his Land Rover lurching towards the road as she picked her way down the short cut into town. It was little more than a cliff path really, but the receptionist had explained that at this time of year it was quite safe, and would take her directly down to the harbour without having to walk back along the road and into the town by the conventional route.

The wind on the cliff face was heavy with salt

spray, Kate could taste it, and the sharp tang of ozone made her feel excited; like stepping out of the train at the seaside when she had been a little girl.

Even the gulls came out to meet her. Or more likely, Kate thought, to inspect the person climbing so close to their private domain. But after several curious swoops they glided away to their rocky perches, from which they regarded her with suspicious, beady eyes—until the novelty wore off.

Francistown had a big harbour, large enough for ocean-going vessels, but today it was deserted. Even the warehouses and dock buildings had a sleepy atmosphere, and Kate wondered if they only sprang to life when ships were in.

She wandered round fairly aimlessly, stepping carefully over chains and shackles and around piles of old crates that had been tied together as if they were some precious cargo. Kate was giving her mind a few moments' rest, allowing her eyes to take in every unfamiliar detail, and it came as a surprise to see suddenly the grand name of *International Petroleum* on the front of a low, tin-roofed building.

She hitched her heavy gadget-bag to a more comfortable position and stared across the narrow street. She couldn't see into the window because a venetian blind had been pulled down for privacy, but it was a safe bet that this was Dougal McInnes' office. Kate felt the terrible temptation to go over for a chat. He might be able to help in some way. Or she could tell him she had met Greg Henderson and he could pass a

CHAPTER THREE

'THEN you'd better think of a way of persuading Greg Henderson to take you out to Sealbank. You've come a long way, lassie, and time's running out!' Dougal McInnes sat behind a cluttered desk, his heavy brows knitted together in displeasure. Kate had finally succumbed to temptation when she had crossed the narrow street and pushed open the frosted glass door, and during the past fifteen minutes she had been explaining her position to him. Well, more or less. She hadn't mentioned Greg's proposition. In fact, the more she thought about it, the more she doubted that he had been serious. They had been words just to frighten her. And now she looked across at the tough engineer, hoping to find a spark of understanding, but there was none.

'You didn't expect this job to be easy, surely?' he continued, flinty eyes flashing in his heavily jowled face, and he glanced at his watch, trying to end the interview without words.

'If only I had more time. If I could be mobile, not dependent on flying out with Mr Henderson. He mentioned Land Rovers. I could get a map . . .'

'That's impossible,' McInnes interrupted. 'We don't have any roads on Drake, apart from those in town and the one out to the airport.' Kate found that hard to believe. Did he think she was expecting a grade one motorway? But there was no sense in arguing now; she'd be able to find out for herself later on. 'So we have to use the Inter-Island service,' he was continuing. 'One of Henderson's flying kites.' You could cut his derision with a knife.

'Is there no other way of travelling round?' Kate persisted.

McInnes sighed, and rummaged through the litter on his desk until he found a typewritten sheet.

'There's the supply steamer that goes round the settlements.' His eye ran down the page. 'But there isn't a sailing until next week, and anyway,' he frowned and tossed the sheet aside, 'you haven't exactly come on a Cook's Tour.' He pointed to her gadget-bag and notepad. 'You've a good enough cover —if no one suspects by your coming here,' he added ominously. 'But you're not really here to take pretty pictures, Miss Lawrence. We want the concession out at Sealbank, and for some reason London thinks you're the person to get it.' He paused, a cruel smile playing around his mouth as he added. 'But don't give up yet. You never know what you might get a man to do—if you offer him enough!' Kate ground her teeth in fury. How right he was!

It must be the Island, Kate fumed later, as she

plodded back up to the hotel. It had to be the Island, the isolation, the lack of feminine company, all contriving to turn the men into evil-minded creatures. It had certainly changed Dougal McInnes, who hadn't even bothered to hide his rough contempt. And for why? They were supposed to be on the same side. Or did he resent London sending him help? And especially for sending a woman?

Well, somehow I'll get that concession, she decided briskly, hurrying as lunch time approached. And I don't need any help from you, Mr Dougal McInnes!

At least the hotel was one ray of comfort in all these proceedings, and Kate was delighted to be out of the wind and restored to its protection. It was small, unpretentious but comfortable, and its owners seemed prepared to fill any role, as Mrs Bryant was now, engrossed in paperwork behind the reception desk.

'I'm glad I saw you,' she said brightly, handing Kate her key. 'The radio station telephoned. They want you to go down to broadcast. That'll be something different to put in your magazine.'

Panic seized Kate by the throat. 'You're joking—broadcast?' There was a sudden vision of *Panorama*, *News at Ten* and *This is your Life* all rolled into one.

'Nothing for you to worry about,' Mrs Bryant assured, not having to be particularly astute to read Kate's mind. 'They always interview visitors. Find out why they're here, and what they think of the place!'

This was getting worse. Kate quickly realised that

Mrs Bryant had said radio station—the Island had no television—but that was still two thousand people *and* Greg Henderson, all listening to her, and she doubted her cover story would stand up to that close an inspection. There would be plenty of experienced photographers hereabouts, not to mention naturalists. The idea of it made Kate go cold. Exposed! And she didn't mean the colour film.

'It's quite informal and they'll make you very welcome,' her hostess continued, glancing at her watch. 'And if you go down after lunch, it'll be their recording session and they said they'd put you down on tape. That'd be better than going out live,' she persuaded, leaning across the counter to pat Kate's arm. 'And you can come back and hear yourself when the programme goes out at eightish.'

Kate tried to talk her way out of it, but when Mrs Bryant began giving her funny looks, Kate gave up and agreed to go. It would probably draw more attention to herself if she didn't conform, and with a bit of quick talking she'd probably come through it all right.

It was only later, halfway through her excellent lunch, that she remembered Greg had said he was going down to the radio station that morning. The food stuck in Kate's throat. Was all this his idea? Was he setting her some kind of trap?

Radio station was perhaps rather a grand description for the little single-storey building that shared its premises with the library.

'I'm afraid they're still recording a schools broadcast,' said one of the young colonial wives, whose interviewing accent would have been out of date even at the B.B.C. 'But he shouldn't be long now,' she continued vaguely, 'and it'll only take a few minutes to get *you* down.' Kate didn't like the sound of that. Did the woman know she didn't have a single thing to say?

They only had to wait in the passageway a few moments, then the red light over the studio door snapped off and almost immediately the door burst open.

'Well, I never, if it isn't our Kate!' Greg Henderson, tall and intimidating, blocked the way into the small room. 'Come for the visitor's spot?' he asked, as if he didn't know; and when the woman confirmed, his expression altered from contrived surprise to wily cunning. 'Now this I must see,' he muttered, turning back into the room. Kate waited for the woman to stop him. But she seemed disinclined to do so, and nearly forgot Kate who was still standing outside in the passageway.

'And when do you hope to see your work in print?' The enunciation was perfect, and Kate stared wildly into the microphone.

The session hadn't gone too badly up till now, with Greg and herself at each end of a table, and the interviewer in between. One wall of the tiny room was a glass partition, and through it Kate could see the technician twiddling knobs.

'I'm afraid I can't give a publication date,' Kate

apologised sweetly, acutely aware of Greg's shrewd eyes behind the veil of curly lashes.

'Have you photographed this kind of assignment before?' she was asked next.

'Ah—similar types of thing,' Kate prevaricated awkwardly.

'I think our guest will find these islands quite unlike any she may have visited in the past,' Greg interrupted. He was off again, and Kate had just about had enough.

'As I'm the guest,' she began haughtily, 'perhaps I can comment with more authority.'

Their interviewer sighed, looked meaningfully through the glass partition, and silently raised her hand, like a film director shouting 'cut'. 'I think it would be best, Miss Lawrence,' she began peevishly, 'if you waited for a specific question before answering. That way we get less trouble editing.' She signalled for a restart and Kate blushed uncomfortably, keeping her eyes away from Greg Henderson's face. The wretched man looked as if he was going to explode, and he didn't even try to keep the laughter out of his voice as he continued explaining about the local wild-life habitat.

Kate seethed inwardly. Oh, he'd arranged this all right. He had everything off just pat. But he hadn't won the round yet, there was still time for Kate to come back fighting.

'And will you be visiting the camp, Miss Lawrence?' she was asked eventually, and if Greg hoped to see Kate at a loss for words he was the one to be disappointed this time. Camp came from the South American word *campos* or countryside. Kate had done her homework and she knew that everywhere that wasn't Francistown the Islanders called camp. Yes, she had every intention of visiting the camp, and she was just about to say so, when the glimmer of a wicked idea materialised. Why not, didn't he deserve it? And as her heart began racing, she said breathlessly. 'Yes, I shall be going out to the camp,' and after only the slightest of pauses, added, 'Mr Henderson has kindly agreed to fly me out to Sealbank!'

The face of the man in question remained a mask, but a hardness came into his eyes, and his full mouth set in a thin line. But their interviewer thought the whole thing quite normal, and she rattled on about hoping Kate enjoyed her visit until the session was over.

Then they were all piling back into the corridor, Greg with his arms full of books, and Kate shrugging herself into her mac, already wishing she hadn't been quite so impetuous. What would Greg say? Why didn't he argue? But then they were outside and Kate, if nobody else, was thankful to escape.

'Want a lift?' Greg offered as he wrenched open the door of his Land Rover, but Kate shook her head and he didn't even try persuading her. She watched the swinging canvas back flap as his vehicle bounced on to the single track road and gradually gathered speed. Then he was out of sight, and Kate began breathing easier.

But relief was shortlived because the temptation

was too great, and Kate just had to listen to the programme when it went out on the air just before dinner that evening. In the privacy of her room Kate could afford to laugh at her awkward mumblings, convinced by now that Greg had ordered her comment to be edited out of the interview. But he hadn't. 'Mr Henderson had kindly agreed to fly me out . . .' It was there. Kate swallowed. Now let him try to get out of that one!

After dinner that evening, Kate drank her coffee in the lounge again, and this time she was joined by the two meteorological men who had flown in with her yesterday. The families of the men whom they were replacing were obviously celebrating their release, and the two wives, who hadn't seen England for four years, pounced on Kate for all the up-to-date details from home. 'Just where *did* one put a hemline nowadays? . . . Oh, the luxury of a really good hairdresser again . . .' Inevitably, the four men began a conversation of their own, and Kate relaxed in pleasant gossip which was a relief after the ordeals of the past couple of days. But then the questions about London gradually swung round to questions about herself. They'd heard her broadcast, and the older woman, a jolly sort with a mischievous twinkle, asked Kate how she had managed to persuade Greg Henderson to fly her out to Sealbank.

'We have our methods,' Kate joked, trying to sound like a well-seasoned reporter, and discounting the sick feeling in the pit of her stomach. If only she didn't have to rely on him for getting her out there. If only she could hire a Land Rover, and then she remembered Dougal's comment, and her own decision to find out the true state of affairs regarding the road situation. Surely there must be *some*!

'No, there aren't,' confirmed the other woman, whose short, dark hair really did look in need of a good hair-cut. 'The upkeep over our kind of terrain would be astronomical. That's why the settlements are all on the coast, so the steamer can reach them with supplies. It's only recently that they've had the benefit of Greg's company, although even that's limited to the places where he can land.'

'And it's quite unusual for him to take—visitors— out there,' the other woman said after hesitating slightly. Visitors, Kate wondered, or had she been about to say *reporters*? But Kate already knew Greg's sentiments about that breed of creature. 'So if we're still around when you get back you will come and tell us all about it, won't you?' she was asked, in a tone that suggested Kate's coming back at all would be a matter for intense surprise.

Kate smiled and made no comment, looking up instead as an elegant blonde strolled into the room. She was tall and had the slim, aristocratic bearing of a thoroughbred filly. As a pint-size brunette herself, such women always made Kate sigh wistfully, and as someone muttered, 'that's the Governor's eldest daughter, Laura,' the woman in question paused and turned back towards the door, waiting for her escort.

It was the second occasion that Kate had heard the
Governor mentioned, and automatically her mind
backtracked to that first time, out in the hall, when
Greg Henderson had picked up the telephone receiver. Therefore her mind was almost ready to
accept the inevitable when he walked into the room
and gently steered the cool, sophisticated Laura towards a secluded table. Kate had been prepared to
see him, the rough-and-ready Greg Henderson who
had presented himself to Kate. But she hadn't been
prepared for the opposition to have become so devas-
tatingly attractive. He was wearing a superb dark suit
that poured itself across broad shoulders, a crisp
white shirt setting off his tan in a most unfair fashion,
and a plain charcoal tie proving he knew no embel-
lishments were necessary. As he passed close by he
nodded to their table, but neither to herself nor anyone else in particular. But Kate, barely returning the
acknowledgement, had noticed his thumb gently
caressing Laura's arm through her pink silky sleeve.
It was in that sensitive crease of her elbow, which
made Kate's similar spot tingle as if he had been doing
it to her.

The men came back into the conversation then;
they all talked about flying and weather conditions,
and someone bought Kate a drink, which was useful
as it gave her something to do with her hands. It was
all very well laughing and joking with such a friendly
crowd, but how was she supposed to act naturally

when she could see Greg out of the corner of her eye? He'd probably sat just there on purpose, giving her an uninterrupted view as he bent affectionately towards his companion, his teeth gleaming as he smiled at her, and his dark chestnut hair glistening from a well-angled table lamp. The peace of the evening was shattered, and he knew it. Would he come across in a minute and say the trip was off? Kate felt breathless, apprehensive, and was annoyed with herself. Okay, so you were wrong and it's unsettled you. Sensible words, but they didn't help. So Greg Henderson *is* used to women, maybe he doesn't have a restricted love-life, but that should make your job easier. But however much she reprimanded herself the feeling wouldn't go away, until Greg and the lovely Laura finally left, and even then Kate's nervousness was replaced by a vague deflation; either way it seemed there was to be no peace.

The party finally broke up a little before midnight and she waved everyone goodbye, with promises to call in for coffee whenever she was passing. Then Kate wandered upstairs and noticed the bathroom was empty as she passed it on the way to her room.

It only took a moment to grab what she needed, and then Kate indulged in a scented, bubbly bath, relaxing away the cares of the day.

Greg Henderson had had two chances, hadn't he? One, he could simply have had her comment wiped out. And two, when he'd seen her again, downstairs, he could have told her there wasn't going to be any trip. It would have been humiliating, in front of the others, but that wouldn't have stopped him. Kate hauled herself out of the bath with reluctance. Maybe he was really going to take her out there, after all. But when?

Kate had been in the bathroom longer than she had intended, and leaving her hair piled high, she hurriedly scrambled into her dressing gown and fumbled with the belt. Then the door stuck and the contents of her sponge bag emptied over the floor as she finally stumbled out on to the landing. Muttering softly, she stooped to gather them together.

'About time!'

Her head flew up. Again her thoughts had seemed to conjure him by magic. 'I—I didn't know anyone was waiting; you should have knocked.' Her fingers trembled as she gathered talcum powder and a jar of face cream that had rolled near his bare feet.

He bent down to beat her to it, and his white towelling robe slipped back revealing a well-tanned knee and muscular thighs. The hairs on his legs were a springy light chestnut. Kate cursed herself for noticing.

'Thank you,' she muttered, without looking at his face, and she heard his mocking laugh at her discomfiture.

'You'll be ready early tomorrow?' he asked, straightening when Kate did, and not attempting to help as she tried stuffing everything back and keep her wretched dressing gown together. 'Seven o'clock okay?' he continued evenly. 'I want to make a reasonably early start.'

Kate hadn't expected him to fly her out so soon. 'That's fine,' she said, forcing herself to meet his eyes. There was that look again; that calculated desire. It might be calculated, but it certainly was effective, and Kate felt her palms go damp.

'What made you change your mind?' he asked, after a moment, and when she obviously didn't understand, he added, 'What made you decide to play the game by my rules, after all?'

Then Kate remembered his proposition that morning. But he'd been joking. He hadn't *really* meant ... Her heart started thudding violently. 'I'm coming out to Sealbank under *my* rules, Mr Henderson. I want that made quite plain,' she managed to say, and his eyes widened at her audacity. 'And there's no point in you arguing,' she continued quickly, 'because two thousand people know I'm travelling out with you. So if you want your reputation as a member of the community to retain its credibility, I suggest you do nothing to upset the delicate balance.' And as a brilliant afterthought, she added, 'I'm sure the Governor would want you to extend the fullest hospitality to a member of the press. I'm sure he'd be most upset if he learned that I'd been treated with anything but respect.'

He wasn't the least impressed with her outburst; in fact such sentiments seemed to make his lips curl in contempt. 'You don't imagine I care one scrap for public approval,' he told her calmly, 'and no amount of Governors would complain at *my* idea of hospitality towards such an enterprising young lady. I said if you came it would be under my rules, and I meant it, Kate. I know exactly how such a visit must end and I'd be a fool if I tried to kid you, or myself, otherwise.'

'Well, then the trip's off,' Kate announced airily, tossing her head and attempting to flounce off down the corridor. But he caught her shoulder with a painful grip and she was forced to turn back and face him.

'But it isn't possible to call off the trip, Kate. You announced it over the air. What help do you think you'll get from other people when they hear you've changed your mind? What will London say when they hear?'

He was nearer the truth than Kate cared to admit. She could almost hear Dougal McInnes gloating.

'I suppose *blackmail* is the only way you can get your women!' she hissed between clenched teeth, almost beside herself with anger.

'Don't you worry your pretty little head how I get my women,' Greg whispered fiercely. Then pinning her back against the wall he continued, 'But you'd better start worrying about what I do to my women, once I get them out there!'

CHAPTER FOUR

'DON'T you try and intimidate me, Mr Henderson,' Kate countered, almost white with rage. 'And if you don't take your hands off me this instant, I shall call for the manager!'

'Oh, good, very good, top marks for spirit, Miss Lawrence.' Greg's powerful hand held her motionless against the wall, but Kate refused to struggle and her bright eyes glowed defiantly. 'And just what will you tell my very good friend the manager?' Greg enquired with such calm self-assurance that Kate could have screamed. 'Will you tell him I object to being manipulated and that I intend teaching our clever little miss here the lesson she undoubtedly deserves? It's about time someone did it, Kate, and as it appears you've chosen me . . .'

'I've done no such thing. Just because I want to take a few photographs . . .'

'Of Sealbank in particular,' he accused, making it all sound highly suspicious—which it was—and Kate lost some of her bounce. 'That's better.' The hand on her waist relaxed slightly and his thumb began gently

stroking the hollow beneath her ribs. 'A lady should
know when to fight, but she should also know when
to stop fighting,' he added, after a slight hesitation.
'The rest, Kate, I'll teach you, believe me.'

Why did his hair have to fall in just that fashion?
—sort of curly at the ends. And why was she thinking about it? Or even caring? Kate knew she had to
get out of this situation fast. 'I am going to bed,' she
announced, breathing in deeply like an affronted
duchess. 'And I shall disregard your impertinent remark, Mr Henderson, but if you forget yourself again
I shall have no alternative but to take the matter further!' She removed his hand with a disdainful flick of
her wrist and waited for him to step back. Then,
exercising superhuman self-control, walked slowly towards her room, with head held high, appearing to
be the cool, calm lady of confidence. But she couldn't
resist sneaking a glance back up the corridor as she
turned to open her door.

And there was Greg, propping himself against the
wall, with one thumb hooked into his towelling belt.
But he didn't look like a man who had just met his
match, nor one that was faintly amused. Either of
those reactions Kate could have understood, but her
brief glimpse had caught him in serious contemplation, and there hadn't been a glimmer of a smile on
his firmly set mouth.

Kate kept up her act until she was safely installed
in her room, then she turned the key, let out a long
sigh and flopped on to the bed. Maybe she should call

off the whole idea while there was still time. If there'd been a plane back to the mainland tomorrow she would have been on it. But it seemed the only plane out tomorrow would be heading for Sealbank, and now Kate tried to imagine just what would be waiting for her out there. But there was no need to imagine because she had all the details, and grabbing her document case, she rifled the contents. At least it was something to do until her unsteady nerves settled.

Dougal McInnes had sent back detailed reports to London over the past eighteen months, and Kate had photo-copies, which told her all she needed to know. Sealbank might be awkward to get to, occasionally cut off, but it was one of the largest settlements on the Island—by comparison, rather like a small hamlet back home. There were several families, each with their own homes; surely she'd be able to make friends with some of them. It wasn't as if the only shelter would be under Greg Henderson's roof.

That much settled, Kate felt somewhat relieved, although she spent another restless night, tossing and turning and thinking about it all. Everything would be all right once she got out there. But it was a conviction that needed clinging to with desperation as Kate waited in the airport's tiny office the following morning.

Greg hadn't changed his mind, and not knowing whether to be pleased or sorry, she eyed him steadily as he filled in countless forms and was handed a weather report ripped off a teleprinter sheet.

Why was this man causing her so much trouble? What was different? Why was this job going haywire before it had even really begun? Had her fingers really trembled, last night, when she'd gathered her bits and pieces together? And had it been because he'd just been there, all hunky, hairy male loosely wrapped in soft towelling? Could an attractive appearance affect her so easily when all the time she knew she hated him? *Attractive*—who said attractive? But he was, in an out-doorsy, wood-smoky, gravelly sort of way. But he wasn't Kate's type. She went for the sophisticated, man-about-town image, and then she had a vision of a girl in pink silk, and the devastating appearance of Greg Henderson on *that* occasion. Kate sighed. It was all so confusing, her mind a jumble of half thoughts, half terrors and delights. What had happened to her comfortable, orderly existence back in London?

'So let's get this baby off the ground!' said Greg, who had wandered up while she had been day-dreaming, and as Kate followed him out on to the tarmac her niggle of apprehension twisted into a tight knot of fear at the sight of his tiny aircraft. She must be mad—out of her mind—but then Greg was helping her to climb up, stowing their bags in the back, and settling himself in the left-hand pilot's seat.

A degree of togetherness was necessary in such cramped conditions, with shoulders touching and arms brushing as Greg leaned across her to flick switches and read gauges. They had both taken off their jackets, and Greg's fitted, pale blue shirt seemed to accentuate his potency as it strained across well-developed shoulders. Kate found his masculinity over-powering at such close quarters, and she only just managed to stop herself reacting when he helped to fasten her seat-belt.

His face was only inches from her own. She could see the texture of his skin in microscopic detail, each individual hair that curled around his ears and the smell of his vital freshness, stronger than the faint hint of aftershave. She was about to abandon her life into his control. If the plane landed safely she would owe him something. The idea was suddenly exciting.

Could he read her mind? Did he know at that precise moment she had never felt more vulnerable? Did something of her inner turmoil show beneath her calm exterior? They met each other's eyes fleetingly. Kate felt like a small animal trapped by a hunter, trapped and held fast, as she was in reality, by strong webbing. Greg ran his hand under the strap, making sure she had room to breathe, and the back of his hand lightly brushing her chest brought an involuntary warmth to her cheeks. She was doing it again, getting all hot and bothered, just as he'd said before. For goodness' sake, get a grip on yourself, girl!

'Have you ever flown in this type of plane before?' Greg asked quietly, still turned towards her, his arm resting on the back of her seat for support.

Did he think she was scared? It was a good way out, and Kate shook her head and shrugged nonchalantly, which seemed to be just the right touch.

'You'll be all right.' He patted her on the head and turned back to the controls, picking up his check-list and immediately forgetting her existence.

You'll be all right—but would she? Was that as far as his comfort went? A gentle pat as if she'd been a pet spaniel. Had Kate expected him to do more than that? She surreptitiously glanced at his stern profile, locked in concentration. Had she wanted him to do more, to kiss her, maybe, to offer with tenderness that which he had only demonstrated in anger up till now? Instead of being shocked by such a discovery, Kate found herself suddenly exhilarated. Just how would he be if he was in love? How would he cajole, persuade, tease? ... But he wasn't in love, at least, not with her. He preferred cool blondes with distinguished connections, and she could picture him escorting the elegant Laura to Government House functions. It was a tantalising vision, this other Greg Henderson, the man his friends saw, because even *he* must have *some* friends. If I wasn't who I am—coming for *why* I am—would it have been different? Would he have shown me his other, friendly side?

The engine sprang to life with a noisy report and it brought Kate back to reality. Forget about that other Greg Henderson, he's only in your imagination. If you hadn't tricked him into this you wouldn't be here now. He isn't interested in you; it's just the plane, the excitement. Kate scolded herself sharply for overreacting. He probably used planes like other men used sports cars—a display of virility, a jet-set passion-waggon. Kate suppressed a giggle, glad that her feelings were coming into proportion and she was seeing the man for what he was. But at least there weren't any convenient laybys up in the sky. He'd have to keep his hands on the controls until touch down or they were both going to be in dead trouble.

Gradually his detached, quiet authority was having a relaxing effect upon Kate, who realised he was taking as much trouble getting this little four-seater airborne as any jumbo-jet pilot would have done.

The propeller was a hazy revolving blur, and the noise was quite deafening, so that when Greg slipped on his headset and spoke into the close-fitting microphone, she couldn't hear a word he was saying as he scrawled something down on his board. Then they were off, taxiing ponderously towards the end of the runway.

'Seat-belt tight?' Greg turned to face her as he stopped again, and Kate realised this was an automatic final check. The fact that he had tightened up her strap a few minutes previously mattered not at all. It seemed Greg, the pilot Greg at any rate, was flatteringly interested in her own well-being.

After another stationary test, when the engine was wound up until everything vibrated, they finally moved out on to the runway and increased speed for take off. The white lines flashed beneath them, until, almost with a cheeky leap, the little Cherokee had left the ground and was pushing its nose skywards, eager for freedom.

Kate didn't have enough eyes to take in everything.

The airfield was gone, lost somewhere behind them, and Greg had banked gently and was heading for the high mountain ridge that had held fascination ever since her arrival.

There was more scribbling, then a fine adjustment of the controls, until the column became feather-light, and he could manipulate it with a finger touch. Then he took off his head-set, glanced into the sky to ensure all was clear, then settled himself as if the hard work was done, and now it was only a question of waiting.

For Kate nothing else seemed to matter but herself and Greg in this throbbing isolation. The ground, with all its problems, was rendered insignificant. Her world, her life, everything, rested in the capable hands of the man on her left. And they were capable hands, that much she had to admit, and although the flight added to his responsibility it reduced hers and left her curiously detached. Her existence, or the end of it, lay completely outside her scope of action. There would be no running faster or jumping back on the curb if disaster struck. Under those sort of conditions what was the point of worrying? So she didn't, and found herself gazing around in wonder, as enthralled with the hazy view of earth as the first men on the moon must have been.

'All right?' Greg had on his metaphorical pilot's cap—the question was purely professional, but Kate was unable to withhold an excited gleam in her eye.

'Fine!' she confessed, having become used to the

noise and finding conversation quite easy with a raised voice.

'We're nearly halfway,' Greg continued, 'see that lake down there?' He pointed to a two-pronged stretch of water. 'Here it is,' he tapped the folded plastic-covered map on his lap. 'We've made good time—the tail-wind's freshened.'

'How can you tell?'

'Number one eyeball,' he said, tapping his cheek with a ballpoint. 'We're just arriving places quicker than my calculation.' He passed over his clipboard and Kate could see the list of E.T.A.s at various landmarks. 'That's the time we should have been arriving,' Greg indicated the first column, 'and there's the actual times we've *been* arriving. There's been a steady increase. But if we'd had a head-wind . . .'

'We'd have been slowed down?'

'Precisely.'

'And you just go by looking?' It seemed strangely archaic. What had happened to all the sophisticated equipment she'd heard about?

'I can fly into Francistown on instruments.' Greg seemed to enjoy the explaining. Was he doing it to make her feel at ease? 'But there's no radar at Sealbank—we have to fly completely V.F.R. out here. So if I can't see, I don't go.' His tone might have suggested, 'Now knock that', but Kate couldn't; it seemed a sensible precaution and, as if she still needed it, further confirmation of Greg's capability.

They increased altitude to clear the snow-capped

mountains with plenty of room to spare. It seemed a wild, inhospitable place below, and Kate found herself beginning to wonder about Sealbank and the problems she would have once they landed—until the sea was visible again in the distance beyond the mountains.

There was no sensation of gradually losing height, but suddenly Kate realised she could see things in more detail, and also, unless Greg intended flying out to sea, he would have to adjust his course. This he now did, the little plane banked to the left, and Greg seemed to have his eye on something below him that Kate couldn't see.

'Seat-belt tight?' The same precision, and Kate realised they were about to land which was rather disconcerting, for at that moment they were sweeping out over the sea. Then Greg levelled the aircraft and reduced speed, and they were coming in over a tiny harbour with a few houses clustered around. Kate couldn't see any sign of an air-strip; she felt her mouth go dry, followed by a sinking sensation in her stomach as Greg made a sharp forty-five-degree turn.

There, just ahead, behind a large, white house, was a tiny, tiny field—with sheep in it! Beyond was a cliff and the wide expanse of ocean. It was the field, plus sheep, or nothing.

Kate glanced at Greg, terrified to make a sound in case she should distract him. He's the one that's mad, she realised. *He* must be out of his mind to imagine he can land a great plane like this on that tiny strip of green.

With their reduced speed, the Cherokee seemed to hang in the air, swinging like a pendulum in the crosswinds. Greg's face was locked in concentration, his hands relaxed on the control column as he gently coaxed the plane on course and dropped it neatly on the grass beyond a low stone wall. The sheep had retreated, the brakes were gently applied, until they were trundling over the bumpy ground towards the house. Now the field looked huge, they hadn't used one half of it to stop, and Kate's fears were being replaced by an intense relief that left her almost light-headed.

The engine was finally switched off—you could practically touch the silence—and Greg turned round to face her. If he had been about to make some comment, he changed his mind, and his stern features slowly broke into a smile as he reflected the expression in Kate's eyes. 'Be careful,' he advised gently. 'You can get hooked, and it's an expensive hobby.'

'You mean I could learn? You'd teach me to fly?' The idea of herself overcoming such obstacles seemed incredible, and made her forget her animosity.

'We'll see.' He was releasing his seat-belt, dismissing the subject, yet his words had been almost indulgent.

Kate stiffly tottered to the ground, her mind a whirl of possibilities, and she sighed, feeling almost happy, as she gazed around at her new surroundings

Greg had brought the plane to rest behind the white house she had seen from the air, and now Kate followed him through a gate in the wall and down a path

that led to the back of the building. The house was
tucked in a hollow, protected on three sides by high
ground, but still retaining a view of the rocky coast
as it continued south in a jagged dog-leg. It was somewhere down there that Dougal wanted his new rig,
but Kate pushed the idea away for the moment. Before they were halfway along the path a black and
white dog hurtled round the side of the house, its
ears flat again its head, a red tongue flapping out like
a banner, its descent on Greg like a thunderbolt.

He put down her case and bent to greet the animal
as a second, and somewhat more sedate version,
trotted in the young dog's wake. Then the greeting
was repeated, Greg had his face washed again, but at
last order was restored and they resumed their pro-
gression towards the back door.

'They stay over with my manager when I'm away,'
Greg explained, searching for his key. 'But when they
hear the plane they know I'm back.' He bent down
and ruffled a shaggy head. 'And I've never yet made it
to the house before this young feller!'

It turned out to be a good way of breaking the ice,
of getting over the threshold and into Greg's kitchen
without that awkward feeling of not belonging. The
Aga had to be inspected, the dogs' water bowls filled,
and the scribble pad on the wall checked for messages.
But there weren't any, and at last Greg turned to face
Kate, resuming the role of host—or was it to be something more sinister? There was a look in his eye that
instantly reminded her of his frightening words last

night. So she was here—and what exactly did Greg Henderson intend doing with her?

But Greg obviously didn't think the time right to demonstrate such intentions, and to Kate's relief she was shown to her room, up shallow stairs and along a broad landing, then down two steps, and Greg had to bow his head as he opened the door.

He put her case on the rug. 'I think you'll find everything,' he said vaguely. 'I'll put the kettle on—coffee?' And one nod sufficed for everything.

Was this really a guest room? Was it the sort of place you'd put a member of the Press of whom you thoroughly disapproved? The bed was a double four-poster, canopied, but in a light, sprigged terylene that matched the curtains and a cushion tossed on to a pink velvet chair. The furniture was dark oak, heavy, and the wardrobe was the sort you climb into and hide. There was several wild-life prints on the wall, a bowl of roses on the dressing-table, fresh pink towels and the smell of polish. Someone had prepared the room recently with love and care, and it showed. Never mind that Greg Henderson hadn't ordered any of these comforts. Someone had. Through the window Kate could see the sun sparkling on distant waves. For the first time since her arrival on Drake it felt like summer.

She found the bathroom and freshened up, feeling strangely self-conscious as she left her toiletries next to the masculine articles lying around. There was soap-on-a-rope hanging by the shower, razors, flat brushes and aftershave. It smelt of sandalwood and shaving cream, and the mixture gave Kate a sensuous pleasure she found difficult to define.

Greg must have heard her coming down the stairs, because he called, 'I'm out here,' and Kate followed the sound of his voice through a low, spacious lounge and beyond, to a long conservatory. She wasn't prepared for it to be pleasantly warm, hot even, and the atmosphere was heady from the intermingling scents of different roses. So this was where they came from. She could believe the elements didn't exactly encourage flower gardens, so apparently the islanders took them indoors.

Kate hadn't been prepared for such comfort, and she certainly hadn't been prepared for the sight of Greg stretched out on a sun-lounger, a dainty china coffee cup looking out of place balanced in such giant hands.

'I've poured yours.' His eyes followed her as she collected it from the coffee table and strolled across to a swinging seat, where she perched uncomfortably on the edge. Then it was her turn to watch Greg as he drained his cup, set it gently down on the floor beside him, and rocked back in the lounger until he was practically horizontal. Then he closed his eyes and began sunning himself as if he was on some South Sea Island cruise.

Charming! But at least Kate didn't have to make conversation. Where were the dogs? Shut in the kitchen, most likely. Unfeeling brute! Then, with nothing else to do, her eyes roved around green foliage, velvety blooms and trailing vines. It really was the nicest place she had discovered lately, and how strange that it had to belong to him. But then how unlikely everything was. Take that silver coffee-pot instead of an earthenware jug. And these cups. Kate surreptitiously turned over a saucer. Spode—she might have known, and she had been expecting heavy mugs. What other surprises did Greg Henderson have in store? And why was he lying there, dormant, like the lull before the storm?

Kate's jumper was sticking to her back; why hadn't she put on a blouse? How long was she supposed to stay here? It was so quiet she could hear a clock ticking out in the hall, a fly buzzing somewhere above her head. Why didn't he say something, do something? Was he waiting for her to make the first move? She started counting window panes to stop herself going mad.

'I'll be going out shortly,' said Greg, before she reached fifty, and she wondered if he'd seen her looking at her watch. She glanced at him quickly, but only now he began opening his eyes in sleepy contemplation. 'I'll be out most of the day going over things with Ralph—that's my manager,' he added, as if she was stupid enough not to realise. 'We'll be getting things organised for the shearing . . .'

Kate tried to listen, but it wasn't any good him talking in such a matter-of-fact way. It was the sight of him lying there, stretched out, in navy trousers

that clung just everywhere. And that shirt, opened
now, halfway down the front, showing little beads of
perspiration that had settled in a gentle hollow. So
he was hot too. Good! Maybe it was the sun, after all,
not this odd sensation beginning again, as it had on
the plane, as it had on that very first evening when he
had stood in her bedroom doorway, all solid, im-
movable, unbeatable male.

Get out of here while you've got the chance. Kate
moved over to the table and replaced her cup. At
least she could still think logically, but was it already
too late? The sleepy eyes watching her began glinting
dangerously; he held out his cup for her to replace as
well, but as she stepped nearer to take it he moved it
away, and again, until she was close enough to be
captured. This he did, swiftly, grasping her wrist with
his free hand, and restoring his cup again to the safety
of the floor. It had served his purpose, and Kate
cursed herself for being so easily duped.

'I'm sure you've a very busy day ahead,' she said as
calmly as possible. 'Don't let me stop you ... You
must have a thousand things ...' But what was the
point of continuing? She might as well knock her
head against a brick wall.

'There's time enough for all that,' murmured Greg,
in such silky accents that it made Kate's skin tingle.
'Why don't you just sit back and relax, enjoy the sun
—maybe I could make room for you here.' Before
she could even try to stop him his hand tightened and
she was forced to perch down beside him. 'That's

better—now I can see you without cricking my neck. And what's all this talk about rushing away? Don't I deserve a rest after flying you out here?' His hand slid gently up and down her arm. She *could* have run away, but somehow it didn't seem like a very good idea. She began breathing quickly, trying to control it, but he noticed, and a gleam of triumph swiftly crossed his face. 'There are those who might think I deserve more than a rest ... Haven't you got what you wanted, Kate? You've arrived at Sealbank. Can't we forget the why or the wherefore?' His smile deepened, and he purred, 'Now come here and thank me properly!'

This wasn't supposed to be happening. Kate should have been thinking of some way of stopping him, some trite remark, but none came.

Greg's languorous mood was catching. It wafted over her like the heady scent of roses, draining away resistance and replacing it with a sensuous tingling pleasure. The fingers on her shoulder gently twisted themselves into her long dark hair, as with eyes and touch Greg coaxed her down towards him. Their lips met, fleetingly, and for a moment common sense made Kate pull back, but his eyes devoured her inexorably and she found the hand behind her head propelling her downwards again.

This time his generous mouth teased away all shyness. She found herself responding, and delighting in such response. This time there was no hint of aggression, as he manipulated with unbelievable expertise.

But suddenly she could no longer marvel or even think as a warm glow softly defused all reality. Then it grew sharper and stronger, demanding more, and getting it.

Greg forced her skirt and jumper to part company, and as a firm, warm hand slid up between her shoulder blades, she wriggled—she just couldn't stop herself. Greg muttered her name softly, she felt his breath warm on her neck, and instinct made her run delicate, hesitant fingers across his chest. The hairs felt damp, his muscular body taut and vitally alive; what on earth was she doing? But she couldn't stop now, and she planted kisses in the wake of each caress as far as she could reach.

But then something made her stop. Greg wasn't participating any more. He was just lying there, his body suddenly rigid. Kate glanced up to meet his eyes uncertainly, ready to smile shyly—perhaps she'd got a bit carried away ... But the looked in his eyes was not what she'd expected, nor his face, tight with control, nor the angle of his chin set with such determination.

'Ten out of ten again, Miss Lawrence,' he whispered in a voice she hardly recognised. Kate couldn't believe such vehemence was possible and she held her breath as he continued harshly: 'I knew you'd be easily diverted, but I didn't think you'd so easily divert *me*. But not now, sweet Kate,' his lip curled, 'I don't have the time to do us both justice.' And he pushed her aside, the lounger rocking precariously as he got to his feet and began tucking in his shirt.

Kate tried to say something, but no words would come and she stared up at him crazily, wondering what on earth he would say next.

'I must apologise for ever suggesting that you don't know exactly what it's all about.' He was working himself up into a fine old temper now. 'And I take my hat off to London.' He strode forward and took her chin in a fierce grip, jerking her face up to meet his. 'Whoever picked you for this job sure knew what they were doing!'

CHAPTER FIVE

'You keep my employers out of this!' At last Kate found her voice, and she came back shouting. 'They wouldn't have sent me down here if they'd known what sort of a man you are . . .' He wasn't letting her go, as if he didn't know, or didn't care, that he was hurting her chin cruelly.

'And what sort of a man am I, Kate? Just because I dislike outside interference . . .'

'Who's interfering, I'd like to know?' she countered without really thinking.

'So would I. You have no idea of the interest that's been taken in us over the past couple of years. Before then, we were left alone to run our own lives. Then suddenly, because we might have something people want, we get one band of cut-throats tramping all over the place, and now——' he paused, finally pushed her away, and swept disparaging eyes over her incensed figure. 'And now we get you turning up, swinging your gadget-bag, if you haven't left it lying around somewhere, suddenly very interested in Seal-bank. Am I supposed to believe it's only for some Sunday supplement? Two unconnected incidents? Well, I don't like being bamboozled, Kate, so don't bring any of your London tricks down here. They won't work!'

'If I had any tricks I wouldn't waste my time performing them on you!' Kate cried indignantly. 'But I notice you've got plenty of tricks up *your* sleeve!' His brows arched in mock surprise and she ranted on. 'Oh, it wasn't wasted, I assure you—the plane trip, all that turning and twirling and feeling relieved to be still alive. It's a good line, Mr Henderson, you should develop it. And then, when the rough edges have been knocked off, you bring me in here.' Her eyes flew around the place. 'Oh, how convenient. Hot, overpoweringly scented—and there just happens to be sun-loungers and swinging seats, and you trick me into coming across for your cup. So don't talk to me about London tricks. I'm sorry if I offended you by kissing you back. It was purely instinct—let's say I was well programmed, but I can assure you it won't happen again!'

'Oh, but it will, Kate, and you know it.' His voice had dropped to a menacing whisper. 'I told you what would happen if you came out here. Admittedly I wasn't prepared for such an immediate reaction. But your display just now, Kate, for whatever motive, leaves me in no doubt that you'll find a repeat performance most acceptable.' The very fact that he could suddenly speak with such icy precision just proved his emotions weren't affected to the slightest degree. She could have cheerfully killed him.

'Well, I wouldn't try proving it—because you'll find it a waste of your time!' Suddenly Kate knew she was going to cry, and before her face crumpled, she tried to push past him. If only she could get to the privacy of her room!

But he caught her and there was no mercy in the cold hardness of his eyes as he stared down at her. Had she ever thought him appealing? It seemed improbable right now. 'I don't have to prove anything, Kate,' he said harshly, 'but you can always try proving me wrong!'

Wrong? Wrong about what? Kate wondered, staring up at him hopelessly. Wrong because she hadn't responded? But she had. Wrong because she wasn't connected with the oil men? But she was. How could you prove a man like Greg Henderson wrong? Everything was stacked on his side. Never had she met anyone she hated more!

'Nothing to say? But of course not.' He didn't quite manage the smile he attempted. 'That's what's going to make it so interesting, Kate. You've got spirit, you'll keep fighting. I wonder how long it's going to take for me to wear you down?'

'I didn't come here to listen to this kind of thing . . .'

'Just what *did* you come for, Kate?' His face was all angular lines as he pulled her roughly against him, but she struggled and broke free, running away through the lounge and, two at a time, back up the stairs. She expected him to follow, but he didn't, which was a relief as there was no key in her lock. Then she flopped down on the bed and had a good howl, which left her exhausted, swollen-eyed and blotchy.

Greg Henderson was an evil-minded ... Kate groped in her pocket for a hanky, an egotistical lout ... there wasn't one, so she fished in her shoulder-bag. He was nothing but a ruthless philanderer ... She blew her nose, sniffed and peered with dismay at her reflection in the dressing-table mirror. But he was right about one thing: she wouldn't give up. And from now on the battle would be waged from a long distance, and the longer the distance between herself and Greg Henderson the better!

The sound of a dog barking finally sent her over to the window and she saw the junior dog leaping and dashing about as it tried to persuade its master to play. She watched dispassionately as Greg threw a stick and stood with his thumbs tucked in his belt, head thrown back with amusement, as the black and white bombshell overran its target and came to a magnificent skidding stop, before snatching up the missile and tearing back with it to Greg. Greg had changed, she noticed. He was wearing cream jeans that looked as if they'd been bleached in the sun, and a brown and cream check shirt rolled up at the sleeves to fit tightly over well-developed biceps. He threw the stick again, this time out of Kate's sight around the side of the house, and soon he disappeared, obviously on his way to see Ralph. But when had Greg come up to change? When she'd been crying? She hadn't heard him—but had he heard her? If so, he hadn't been exactly forthcoming with the comfort. But then that was the last thing she would have wanted.

Now that the house was empty, she could breathe more easily. She unpacked steadily, had a shower to revive her spirits as much as anything else, and left her smart skirt and sweater in the wardrobe; this was definitely the place for jeans.

Then, with curiosity getting the better of her, she went downstairs and wandered around. She liked the general impression of elegant comfort, parquet flooring or delicately patterned carpet, dark, polished furniture, or heavy, comfortable chintz-covered couches. The dining room, like the kitchen, was at the back of the house, overlooked by the mountains, and on its walls were several wild-life sketches. There was one of an adorable baby seal, another of a drunken penguin and a third of a heron struggling with an oversize fish. There was a hint of humour in all of them that appealed, and Kate found herself smiling as she went into the kitchen to make herself a cup of coffee. The ancient dog was still curled up in its basket and as Kate entered it opened one eye, thumped its tail to denote approval, and promptly went back to sleep. At least, she thought, there was someone at Sealbank who didn't object to her drawing breath!

She took her coffee through to the lounge, picked up a six-month-old copy of the *National Geographical* magazine that happened to be lying around, and made herself comfortable on one of the huge settees. But as lunch time approached she began to feel unsettled again.

Yet she needn't have bothered. When Greg returned he stayed barely five minutes. He'd be having a working lunch with Ralph, he told her. He just wanted to try the radio, and he left Kate standing in the hall to where the sound of his arrival had summoned her. On first seeing him she had felt selfconscious, but Greg showed no sign of even remembering their recent encounter, and if he had heard her crying it certainly wasn't bothering him now.

She was intrigued with his urgent, something's-in-the-air manner, and why bother with the radio? But as he left his study door slightly ajar she realised he wasn't exactly tuning in to the local chat-show. He seemed to be calling someone, muttering impatiently and flicking switches; but apart from a few strange oscillations, he got no response. When Kate heard him snap off the apparatus she hurried back into the lounge, grabbing the magazine again and nonchalantly flicking the pages.

'You'll get yourself something, then,' Greg said from the doorway. It was an order rather than a question, and Kate acknowledged with the merest inclination of the head. Greg grunted, which might have meant approval or scorn, but as he turned away he suddenly seemed to remember something, and Kate looked up, knowing instinctively that he was about to speak. 'We've been invited out to dinner tonight. Eight o'clock—you'll be ready?' And then he was gone, to the accompanying scurry of paws.

It was the last thing Kate had expected. Was this his way of saying sorry? Would a man like Greg Henderson ever feel the need to say sorry? Two questions to keep her mind fully occupied as she spent the afternoon getting to know Sealbank.

She photographed the house, its bricks painted white, the tiled roof a mellow, reddish brown, and the long conservatory a riot of colour all down one side. There wasn't much of a garden, a few hardy shrubs, some vegetables growing behind a sheltering wall, and Kate found an outhouse stacked with blocks of peat ready for winter fires. The path at the side of the house ambled downwards, crossing a stream where large boulders had been placed for stepping stones. Then up again, the other side; the grass short and springy with white rocks protruding at intervals, looking as if they had been scattered long ago and their collection again would be just too much trouble. At the top of the next rise Kate could look down on the settlement proper. It was inland, to her left, with half a dozen houses, a large barn or something, pens, the sound of machinery, men and dogs. But Greg would be down there and she was in no mood to meet him, so she took the right-hand fork, down towards the sea and a jetty snuggling in the protection of the headland. It wasn't exactly the harbour she'd imagined from the air, but this would be where the steamer tied up, the steamer that brought provisions and took away the produce, the steamer that Dougal had told her about. When would it get here? Next week—the week after? But even such a tenuous link with escape she found comforting.

She kept to the coast, climbing over slippery rocks running with water. Then she was the other side of the inlet, as high as Greg's house, and she could sit down and look back at it all. And then she began to worry.

'Look,' she told herself firmly. 'Two days ago you didn't have a hope of getting out here—but here you are. Big John would be impressed, anyone would be impressed. You're back on schedule. Think positive. Now, in the next couple of days, you have to bring the question round to oil. You've done it before,' she continued boldly. But somehow this trip was different. It wasn't so easy to think objectively. Before, there had been reports, statistics, common sense, whereas now . . . She closed her eyes and tried to dispel the image that kept coming to her mind. She kept smelling roses, and seeing a big, vital man with warm, nut-brown eyes that for ten whole minutes had sent her crazy. Kate had never known anything like it. To be kissed was one thing, but in that particular way; passionately but with tenderness; deeply but without aggression. Greg had coerced a response from her bottomless pit, her innermost, secret self. In fact, so secret was the place that Kate hadn't known it existed. Until Greg had shown her. It made the day somehow special.

But what she'd got to remember was that other look in his eyes. When they weren't a warm nut-brown. When they were cold and hard, like those rocks down there, and just as treacherous. Then his whole being had changed from spontaneous lover to dominant overlord. To outside interference, to meddlers, there would be no quarter given. So just what would happen in these next few days when she did bring the question around to oil? Could she shout 'help' to Dougal? Could he do anything? Would he even want to? If things became that bad he might think it was to Inpet's advantage to disown all knowledge of Kate. Like a real spy; she shivered at the prospect. Only this one was well and truly stuck *out* in the cold ...

Ralph and Jean West were the kind of people Kate took to immediately. She knew that the moment the tall redhead opened the door to them that evening. She guessed they were both a goodish bit older than Greg. Ralph all wiry, bronzed, with a shock of prematurely grey hair. And Jean, with a good figure and a pleasant, welcoming smile when they had arrived.

Kate caught Ralph watching her on several occasions during dinner. If he'd spent the entire afternoon with Greg had they only discussed the farm? Could Kate have been a topic of their conversation as well? But she pushed the idea away. If Ralph West disapproved, he wasn't letting it spoil his wife's obvious pleasure at having a guest from the outside world.

'I *am* glad I insisted you both come to dinner,' said Jean, collecting the empty dishes of their main course. 'I knew she wouldn't be tired, Greg. And the mood you're in you'd have been no company for a visitor.'

Imagine telling him off like that! But Jean got away with it; Greg even gave her a smile, but it had vanished when he looked across the table at Kate. 'You see, this wasn't my idea,' his eyes seemed to say. 'I'm only doing it for Jean.' And Kate felt a little stab of disappointment in her heart.

'I suppose there's still no news,' Jean continued, bustling in again with a chocolate gateau and lashings of thick, frothy cream. Kate looked blank and Jean tutted. 'Hasn't Greg told you?' Then she glanced at her husband before continuing. 'It's one of the shepherds, Tom, he's supposed to radio in at regular intervals. But we haven't heard from him today . . .'

'It's probably nothing,' Greg broke in.

'Is that who you were trying to reach at lunch time?' Kate asked, and he nodded.

'We thought there might be something wrong with Ralph's equipment. It's best to check.'

'Have you tried since?' Jean asked the two men, handing round plates piled high with calories.

'Ralph tried this afternoon, and I had another go now, just before we came out.' He dug his fork into the elaborate concoction and paused with it halfway to his mouth. 'I expect the wretched boy's just forgotten—or broken his set. There's no need to panic unnecessarily—and there's nothing we can do tonight, anyway.' He sounded as if he was convincing himself as much as anyone.

Kate insisted on helping Jean while the coffee percolated, and their note of conversation was somewhat more jovial than the preceding hour and a half's. If Jean noticed the underlying tension between Kate and Greg she tactfully didn't mention it.

'Do you find it rather lonely living out here?' Kate asked, loading the dishwasher, or at least trying to.

'Not really, it's a way of life,' Jean began, arranging cups and saucers on a trolley. 'People are important—and families. I miss the boys terribly, of course . . .' And Kate felt awful because it just hadn't occurred to her. Then Jean went on to explain that their two boys were at boarding-school in Francistown. 'Janice is coming up seven, so she's still at home. I teach her what I can—we have a sort of travelling tutor who comes round every so often.' She nodded towards the radio. 'And of course, there's the school of the air. But I suppose she'll be off in three or four years' time.' Jean shrugged and smiled. 'But that's how it is. You have to accept it. But some things are worth the sacrifice.'

Some *things* or some *people*? wondered Kate. Would Jean have settled with Ralph on the moon if he'd wanted her to go there?

Then Jean changed the subject to Kate's visit, and soon they were wheeling in the coffee trolley and Kate was selecting a seat as far away from Greg Henderson as politeness would permit. If it was a question of going to the moon, he'd have to make the trip alone. Imagine getting stuck up there with him!

'I've just been talking to Kate about this project of hers,' said Jean, settling herself near the blaze her husband had kindled in the stone hearth. 'And I don't care what either of you say,' she continued. 'If Sealbank's going to be in a magazine I think it's all very exciting!'

Kate shifted uncomfortably in her seat, glad that the lighting was subdued and that stirring cream into her coffee gave her something to do with her hands. Ralph got up to pour brandy, and Jean went over to the tape deck to select some music. It was all very informal, a friendly, family occasion, with soft firelight and Jacques Loussier gently improvising Bach. But Jean's remark proved they had all discussed the probabilities. But only Jean had judged, and found Kate innocent. She looked across and caught Greg's swift appraisal, and there was nothing soft and friendly about *his* judgment as firelight danced off the hardness in his eyes . . .

There wasn't any moon that night, and Greg led the way back home, up the narrow path, blocking out the sky and stars for Kate whenever she glanced upwards. But there was something comforting about his broad back and easy strides that made walking in such spooky stillness almost a pleasure. The vision of Jean and Ralph, waving goodbye from the warm glow of their house, had made Kate feel strangely sad. Wouldn't it be nice if she was returning to such domestic comfort!

She hastily put the idea aside, then stumbled over

a loose rock and fell against the man of whom she had momentarily wished so much. He was wearing his tweedy jacket again and it tickled Kate's nose. Then he was turning round, steadying her, his face lost in darkness, but she could feel his breath drifting across her forehead.

'All right?' he queried, and Kate wished she could have felt as calm as he sounded. He kept hold of her hand after that, it felt warm and strong; but it was only because they'd reached the stream, and once they had negotiated it he went ahead again, leaving her to follow behind like a well-trained mongrel.

But maybe it hadn't been such a bad evening, on the whole, broadly speaking . . . Kate tried to talk to herself nonchalantly, but a disquieting feeling began creeping into her mind. If this had been purely a social trip, with Greg as friendly towards her as he was towards Jean, wouldn't she really be enjoying herself by now? She didn't care to analyse the subject further, so she pushed it to one side, although a general feeling of edginess prevailed.

When they reached the house Greg put the dogs out and pottered about for ages so there was nothing for Kate to do but say goodnight and go up to bed. But it was a flat ending to the evening. There should have been something more, although she couldn't decide quite what.

Did even Greg get up at five-thirty in the morning? Kate peered at her wrist watch, groaned and rolled over, trying to go back to sleep. But then a door slammed, someone was running from the house, and someone else was marching about downstairs with little regard for sleeping visitors. Immediately Kate knew something was wrong, and she was out of bed, groping for her dressing gown and stumbling out on to the landing.

'What's happened?'

Greg was gathering a pile of gear on the kitchen table—food, medical supplies, blankets. 'It's Tom.' He didn't seem in the least surprised to see her. 'He's sent a message through at last. Had a bit of an accident —broken his leg, he thinks—and we've got to go out and bring him back.' Greg's gruff, early morning face stared across the table, and there was an aggressive, no-nonsense set to his shoulders that Kate found rather disconcerting. 'It'll be a long trip,' he continued, 'come with me and I'll show you,' and Kate was obliged to run after him as he strode towards the study.

She hadn't included the study in her tour of inspection yesterday. It was a private room, *his* room, yet she was curiously pleased to have the excuse now.

The room was smaller than she'd imagined. There was a bookcase, but the volumes were well worn. There was the radio transmitter; and a large mahogany desk, both needing dusting. Whoever came in to clean obviously wasn't allowed to touch them. There were no comfortable armchairs or giant globe on a stand, instead there were rows of lever-arch files, looking as if they went back many years.

Stock lists, veterinary-looking instruments in polythene bags and some sort of silver cup that might have been presented at an agricultural gathering. There were photographs on the wall, both of sheep and cattle, framed certificates that Kate couldn't read without getting closer, and one out-of-place picture of a tiny aeroplane flying upside-down at a display. Kate took all this in as she crossed to a wall where a large-scale map had been pinned.

'This is Sealbank,' Greg waved a hand unnecessarily. 'Francistown is up here.' He tapped the wall, way off the map. 'You can see,' he went on, 'that we're completely cut off from the rest of the island by those mountains.' His finger ran along the ridge they had flown over yesterday. 'All the land this side of the mountains belongs to me.' He wasn't bragging, just stating a fact, and Kate wondered how long his family had owned the settlement. It must have been for several generations for him to accept it so calmly.

'We have to go up here.' Greg pointed to a spot north-west of the settlement. 'The replacement's already started out. He's taken a good horse; he'll probably reach Tom before we do. So come on.' He looked down at Kate's dishevelment. 'You'd better go and get dressed, it's going to be a long ride.'

'But surely you don't need me,' Kate protested. 'I'm not a nurse, what help can I be?'

Greg laughed unexpectedly. 'I don't expect you to be any *help*. In fact, I imagine you'll be a thundering nuisance.' He looked about to elaborate, then seemed to change his mind. 'But I can't leave you here, so go and get dressed—we're just wasting time arguing.'

'I'm perfectly capable of looking after myself for a few hours,' Kate retorted angrily.

'Few hours!' Greg passed a hand over his face, and when she could see it again there was a curious expression behind the impatience.

'Kate!' He came across and rested heavy hands on her shoulders. 'Kate, there are half a dozen lads in the bunk-house out there.' He might have been explaining the facts of life to an eight-year-old. 'They haven't seen—anyone like you,' he continued after a slight hesitation, 'for many, many months. Your spirit may be unwilling, Kate,' the corners of his mouth twitched, 'but their flesh will be anything but weak. You're coming with me, my girl, and no nonsense.'

Kate's cheeks felt as hot as her shoulders beneath his touch. 'I can go and stay with Jean.'

'She's got enough to do without playing nursemaid to you.' His eyes flashed challengingly.

'I can look after myself, then.'

'With my lads?' he snorted. 'I doubt it.'

'So what makes you so different? If I wouldn't be safe with them, how do I know I'll be safe with you?'

'You don't!' It was the only reply possible, but Kate felt like wiping the supercilious smile off his face. 'But I have more freedom than they do. Let's say I can afford to be more—selective. And then there's only one of me, Kate.' The pressure near her neck increased for a second. 'You can always try fighting me off. But with the boys . . .' He trailed off, shaking his head despondently, as if her battle with them was already lost.

Kate pouted angrily and wriggled free from his grasp, but the only place she could go was backwards, until the solid desk stopped even a partial retreat.

Greg knew there was no way she could leave the room until he chose to allow it, and as they stared at each other she saw his taunting expression subtly change to something more sinister.

'Well, I'm just not going,' she announced haughtily, as much to break the sudden tension as anything else.

'But it isn't up to you, Kate.' His eyes nearly swallowed her up. 'I'm the one who makes the decisions. And I won't have you staying here alone, poking about, asking questions.' His eyes glinted as he added forcefully, 'I want you where I can see what you're up to—twenty-four hours a day!'

And you didn't argue with a man when he stood less than two feet away, looking so strong, so unbeatable, so absolutely determined to have his own way.

reserved for Laura. Well, she was welcome to him.

Kate marched back upstairs, glancing angrily at Greg's open bedroom door as she passed by and heard him moving around inside. He couldn't actually force her to go—so she hurried into her own room and dived under the bedclothes.

How long would he be gone? A day? Maybe two? What heaven! And she tried to relax in her dark cocoon although any moment expecting Greg to burst into the room ranting and raving. But he didn't come—yet—and after another five minutes she heard him go downstairs. So she started rehearsing all the terrible things she would eventually say to him. But no words came, and only one face swam before her—and it wasn't Greg, or even Laura, which was surprising. It was Dougal McInnes, and she could almost hear the thick rasping of his breath as she remembered his anger and cruel denouncement. 'You're not on a Cook's Tour,' he had reminded her, and now the words returned to torment. It wasn't supposed to be easy, she wasn't supposed to be enjoying herself. The kind of trip Greg had in mind would be pure torture, but wouldn't it give her a unique opportunity? He would certainly have to listen to her if they were cooped up all day in the same vehicle. When would she get his undivided attention again?

Groaning, she struggled up, pushing back the covers and ruffling her tangled hair thoughtfully. Okay, Mr Greg High-and-Mighty Henderson, I'll come with you—but only because I want to! And as she started flinging jeans and sweaters into a pile, she wondered if Big John would ever realise the sacrifices she was making on his behalf.

Low cloud was rolling down the mountain, shifting and swirling, revealing cracks and crevasses one moment and then wafting them away with its magic, misty curtain. The morning was damp and chill, and the air was heavy with moisture so that Greg had to keep the wipers switched on. And it wasn't exactly a summer mist that precedes a very hot day. This was the bone-chilling, teeth-chattering version.

Had Kate thought the trip might last a couple of hours? At this rate they would be lucky if they did it in a couple of weeks. She clutched the dashboard as Greg lurched into a pothole, fighting a spinning wheel, and then they were straight again and lumbering onwards. The last mile had taken twelve minutes, Kate had timed it. There might not be any roads on Drake, but she hadn't expected the going to be this rough without them. There was nothing ahead but mountains, while behind and around them the country stretched away into flat, greyish wilderness.

Sealbank seemed a hundred miles away, and Francistown could have been on another planet. A huge bird hovered in the sky near the mountains and they could see wild cattle grazing in the distance. The further they travelled the more Kate realised the complete isolation of the island. In Francistown one could almost forget this was the South Atlantic Ocean.

There was talk of the Governor, and a middle-class colonial society adhering rigidly to the traditions of home. But here, bouncing along in a mud-spattered vehicle, with a tough, determined man who was used to people jumping when he commanded, she could readily believe that civilisation stopped on the other side of the mountains. Hadn't she once thought that coming out here would be like stepping into the lions' den? And this lion's den was more than just Sealbank, this was his territory—and his rule was absolute. She glanced at him momentarily, seeing his outward toughness yet sensing something far more dangerous beneath his exterior. Within him a fire smouldered. Occasionally she had seen it flicker to the surface, but up until now he had managed to keep the flames well doused. But would it always remain so when she started talking to him about the oil? It seemed un-likely, so once more she put off the awful moment. But the time would have to come soon—and just what on earth would she say . . .?

After a few moments of fruitless thought she let her eyes waver his way. *He* wouldn't be frightened at the prospect of being out here alone. His ramrod legs were clad in cord jeans today, and a green check shirt collar sat comfortably over a heavy ribbed sweater. Whatever he did he seemed to fit the part. Today he almost blended into the scenery, or maybe he *was* the scenery, as much a part of this island as the rocks and rivers and mountain streams.

Except for couple of short breaks they drove on until eightish, when the cloud came rumbling in again and they could tell it was going to get dark early.

'This'll do,' said Greg. And 'this' was a reasonably level stretch of springy grass beside a river, or was it a stream? When did one become the other? But Kate was too tired to ask. And there were the tents still to be put up, and supper to be cooked—and, oh dear, hadn't it been a long day?

The first problem came when Greg said, 'We'll put the tent there.' *Tent*—singular? Okay, so perhaps he preferred to sleep in the truck. They only just set it up before the rain returned, and Kate plonked on her red P.V.C. combat hat. But the rain dripped off its brim and ran down her nose, and she wiped it away with the back of her hand as Greg hammered in pegs and adjusted the guys. Then it was backwards and forwards with the gear, and 'Keep it dry!' he called out. Oh, very funny, but Kate did her best and at least he didn't shout at her. And then, heaven be praised, he started cooking.

They ate their meal in the tent. It was an extremely small tent really, just one lilo long by two lilos wide, and they perched on a pile of bedding, muddy boots left in the doorway, the steady patter of rain on terylene almost soothing.

'Will we get to Tom tomorrow?' asked Kate, as her eyelids grew heavier and Greg took her plate before she dropped it.

'Hard to say.' She noticed him studying her carefully. 'With luck we'll make it. Let's hope everything goes our way.'

'Mm.' Kate was warm and sleepy and the sound of

his voice was mixed up with a comfortably filled tummy, the softness of warm sleeping bags beneath her, and the gathering gloom as night came in fast.

'Bed?' Greg suggested, offering to go and wash up while she undressed. And it was only when she was slipping into her nightie that she realised this wasn't exactly the most suitable garment to wear. Maybe I should have borrowed a pair of pyjamas, she grinned impishly. But then he probably didn't wear pyjamas. She was suddenly tense inside and half afraid to wonder why.

'Okay?' came Greg's voice from outside. He hadn't taken long, and Kate quickly scrabbled into an anorak.

'I've shifted all my things,' she muttered suspiciously, feeling slightly more respectable with something around her shoulders. 'I don't know which is yours . . .'

'You have the green bag, it's warmer,' he said, when he was inside and almost filling their confined space. Then to Kate's astonishment he began to slowly peel off his sweater. It was her expression that stopped him going further.

'If you think you're sleeping there you can just think again!' she announced indignantly, suddenly wide awake and very wary.

'And if you think I'm sleeping out in this downpour,' Greg retorted with a sigh, 'then you're the one who can think again.'

'Well, if you won't, I will.' Kate tossed her head

and scrambled to the stooping position necessary under the low ridge. She grabbed the nearest bed-bag and tried to make her escape.

'Where do you think you're going?' Greg was suddenly angry as he pulled her away from the entrance and toppled her on to his lilo. 'If you set one foot outside everything will be drenched. The sleeping-bag stays in here.'

Kate glared at him mutinously, but there was only hard resolution in his eyes. 'If you were a gentleman you'd sleep in the Land Rover,' she managed to say in a strangled sort of choke. Oh, why did he make the most simple of things such an ordeal?

'Like hell I will,' came the quick reply. 'Don't be ridiculous, Kate. That cab leaks like a sieve, there's no rear window, the wind will come straight in from the back.' The gas light cast stern masculinity into angular shadows. 'I've a hard day's driving tomorrow and I need a good night's sleep. I'm sleeping there.' He pointed to where she had fallen. 'You can stay there if you like, or you can move over. Either way I don't very much care. And *if* I was in the mood for a bit of ravishing, which by God I'm not,' he added hastily, 'I'd choose someone . . .' He broke off, not wanting to admit . . . but Kate knew exactly who he would choose. 'This isn't the time for maidenly indignation,' he continued firmly. 'We've got to stay dry—and we need some sleep. Now, get out of my way,' he ordered, rolling her over and rearranging the sleeping-bag.

'You can keep your sleeping-bag—and you know what you can do with it!' Kate struggled up again. 'But you can't stop *me* going outside.' Afterwards she wondered if that was a challenge she had hoped he would take up. But he didn't, and to get out she had to scramble over him in an extremely undignified manner.

'You'd better wear this.' No protest, no last minute, gallant act of moving out, Greg handed her his parka. 'You can't go out there—in such a thin nightie—with such a short jacket . . .' His innuendo was perfectly clear and Kate cursed herself for blushing. 'Go on—take it. Where you're going you'll need it.' He sat up, still outside his sleeping-bag, the gas light swinging above his head making mobile shadows now.

Kate shrugged herself into the jacket which came down past her knees, and then pulled on her shoes. She knew she looked a fright, but was past caring. Then she was struggling with the entrance flap while he just lay there, watching, looking so smug with two sleeping-bags while she went out into the night.

'You'd better put this thing on, as well.' He reached across and crowned her with the red plastic hat. 'And Kate.' He caught her arm, his voice sharp as he spoke her name. 'You can go,' he added rationally when she struggled. 'But later—when you've cooled off—come back.'

'You don't think I'm setting foot——' she began, but was silenced with a firm finger against her lips. Greg's face was suddenly very close, very disturbing. He was so vitally alive—so male.

'Don't stop out there just to prove a point,' he was saying. 'It isn't worth it. It's going to get extremely cold, and very lonely. I'll give you half an hour—an hour at the most.' Then he lay back and stretched luxuriously, surrounded by softness and warmth.

'I'll see you at breakfast,' Kate retorted, unzipping the tent and trying not to catch the all-knowing, all-powerful expression in his eyes. It was no good him sounding reasonable when he looked so devilishly self-assured and quite lethally handsome.

The cab did leak—but a drop of rain never hurt anybody. The draught blew in from the back—but fresh air was good for the complexion. Kate could take it—for the first twenty minutes, anyway. It wasn't really the gear-stick in her ribs that stopped her dropping off to sleep, nor was it the rain sounding like half a dozen armies in full retreat stomping over the roof and bonnet. Perhaps if she just sat up for a bit, got really tired, so she leaned against the driving wheel and peered through the rain-distorted windscreen.

And then she heard it. A sort of bark—or was it a roar? And then splashes. Heavens, something was out there! She wound down the window and peered out, and the noise came again, but louder. Whatever it was seemed extremely close. There was something in the river ... Was she seeing things or was there a blur moving ...?'

'*Greg!*' Her voice was little more than a squeak and her fingers shook as she battled with the stiff catch and practically fell out of the truck. Hadn't she sworn not to go back until morning? Never mind her pride when her life depended on it.

'Greg,' she croaked, shaking him roughly, but he only moaned and snuggled down deeper. 'Wake up!' Rain dripped off her hand and landed on him. 'There's something out there!' And at last he rolled over and opened his eyes.

'Honey, you're soaking me . . .' Then it appeared he didn't seem to mind too much, and an arm, a bare arm, she noticed with alarm, snaked out of the sleeping bag and around her neck. 'Take that hat off,' he whispered softly, but she couldn't waste time listening to any of that—didn't he realise . . .

'There's a great—great *thing* out there,' she blustered. 'It must have been on the bank—now it's in the river—and it's making a terrible noise!'

Greg unzipped his quilt and was outside in a couple of seconds, motioning to Kate to stay where she was. But she wasn't letting him out of her sight.

'It was over there,' she said, stumbling after him and pointing with an unsteady hand. Didn't he know he was getting wet standing out here in just his cords? Wasn't the rain freezing on his bare shoulders? Where was his jacket? And then she realised she was still wearing it.

'I don't see——' Greg was beginning, and then it came again, another roar, and Kate clutched his arm, waiting, but 'Oh!' was all he said.

She wasn't impressed. 'What—what is it?' she implored, feeling a slight tremor run through him.

'Ah—seals,' he replied evenly.

'Seals!' And she had a vision of adorable babies, like the sketch on his dining room wall. Or circus seals, well groomed and civilised. But there was nothing civilised about the brute out there.

'Elephant seals, actually,' Greg continued, sounding quite serious now. 'They're pretty big fellows—we're probably on their territory. You never can tell.' And this remark was punctuated by a lot of thrashing about and wild exchanges. Now there were at least two of them. 'I don't think you'd better stay out here alone,' he continued, firmly taking Kate's arm and steering her towards the tent. 'They'll probably be all right . . .'

'Wouldn't it be safer in the truck—off the ground?' Kate suggested, not really caring where she was, so long as Greg was right beside her. Now was the sort of time for his kind of strength to come in handy.

'The truck would be far more dangerous.' He hesitated. 'We've got the supplies in there. They're more likely to nose around where there's food.'

'You mean, like bears?' asked Kate, staring up at him, wide-eyed. Everyone knew about bears and rubbish tips. Of course seals—great elephant seals—would be just the same.

'Exactly!' He was helping her scramble back into the tent, then finding the matches and giving her some light. 'So if we just sit tight—and keep quiet,' he added with meaning, and then he was gone again before she could retort.

I suppose he is serious—they are really dangerous, she thought. But it was only a fleeting thought, and soon she was shrugging off his great jacket and slipping into the sleeping-bag he had left open for her. And then all her doubts vanished when Greg returned.

'Just in case,' he said, laying a giant spanner beside the flap so that it could be used as a weapon if the necessity arose. Then the commotion began again outside, so Kate stayed awake for ages, listening to the raucous excitement of the colony. There seemed to be loads of them now, and they were patrolling this stretch of river most enthusiastically. Greg soon fell asleep and she realised she had been hearing his slow, regular breathing for some time. His solid bulk between her and the entrance was the sort of comfort that finally allowed her to relax sufficiently and doze. But not for long. Suddenly she was awake, and the noise outside was awful. She sat bolt upright, straining to hear a movement on the grass and the first tremble of the guy ropes.

'It's all right, honey,' said a sleepy voice beside her, and there was something in the way he said, 'honey', that caused her pulse rate to quicken. 'They won't hurt you,' he reassured her, and his arm came out again to coax her down.

'They—sounded—close.' She was trembling, lying down again as he was demanding, and it wasn't the seals she was frightened of now. There was something so inevitable about the way Greg was handling her;

firmly, positively, as if he was instinctively aware that she wouldn't resist. 'What time is it?' she asked quickly, hoping that if he looked at his watch he would at least have to take his hands off her.

'Lord knows.' So that didn't work, and he was bending over her now, his head silhouetted against the early glow of dawn. 'It's pretty cold—are you warm enough?' he asked, touching her nose, which was icy, and her chin, and then he was snaking a hand around her neck, feeling the sensitive skin of her shoulders.

'I—I could do with a sweater,' Kate managed to say in a fairly normal voice. It was just possible to see the contours of his face gathering shape in the soft grey light. His eyes glinted and the sensuous curve of his mouth was outlined in a deeper shade of grey.

'Mine's nearest,' he said at last, groping beyond his pillow for the ribbed sweater he had worn yesterday, and as Kate struggled up he lay down on his back, his hands propped behind his head, and she could feel his eyes watching her as she pulled the sleeves the right way out. Was it her turn to be silhouetted now? Even a soft light could play tricks. But everything was all right until she raised the enormous sweater above her head, and then, in that vulnerable moment when it was neither on nor off, she heard Greg's sudden intake of breath.

'I've got a better idea for keeping you warm,' and the words came from deep in his throat, like the awakening roar of a wild animal. Then he was suddenly snatching the sweater away, tossing it into a darkened corner, and Kate was staring wildly into eyes than danced with a devilish light. 'Come here and let me show you,' he whispered huskily.

His sleeping bag was already unzipped, and this time, as he propelled her downwards, he made sure she landed on his side.

'No, Greg, please . . .' Her hands pushed against his shoulders in a useless gesture of protest.

'You know you don't mean it . . .' His breath was warm against her neck as he eased her out of her sleeping bag, swearing softly as she struggled.

'Greg, you can't—not like this . . .' But his lips closed on hers with a force and strength of will that was overpowering. She felt her arms draw him closer, her fingers wind into his tousled hair and she was being slid sideways into his open bag. Her bare legs touched the warmth that had surrounded him all night and then he pulled the top over both of them. She was really in a man's bed for the first time, and excitement brought sensitivity to even the touch of smooth nylon.

Kate Lawrence, what have you got yourself into now? But she knew—anyone would know—and Greg was so positive—so sure. But how could he be? How could he know? But it was so warm and beautiful, and did she really mind his hand meandering down to her breast, where it lingered awhile before going lower, as it was now, sliding over smooth skin . . . She automatically flinched and he immediately stopped in his tracks, coming back up to her mouth and coaxing with long, lingering kisses. It was so much more effective when he was gentle; it spread a warm glow—and it started a dull ache so that next time his lips and hands explored her body, she didn't resist.

'You couldn't have expected me to just lie there,' Greg was saying, 'not with you wearing just this,' and he held up a handful of lemon nylon for her inspection. 'Honey, I'm not made of stone,' and how right he was! Kate could feel the life throbbing through him. His hard, muscular body pressing urgently against her own, but it wasn't cold to the touch, her fingers gripping his back told her otherwise. 'That's my girl,' he muttered, his eyes flashing with the desire he knew she was sharing.

'I'm not your girl!' It still seemed necessary to fight him, but only verbally now, her body was reduced to thrilling tingles as he found a beautifully sensitive spot.

'You will be in a minute,' he said softly, his breath irregular now, and she was frightened. Frightened because she wasn't frightened. She wanted him *now*. Not later—not maybe if he loved her—but this minute, and the shame of it was overwhelming. So now she really knew how he coaxed and cajoled, and he sure was good at it. She had never let anyone get this far before. But it wasn't a question of letting—of choosing to allow him. She had no say in the matter —with spectacular hands and lips Greg intruded magnificently.

'We don't want this,' he murmured, beginning to pull the nightdress over her head. But she resisted and he looked down at her with amusement. 'Honey, it can't make any difference—and with the kind of romp we're going to have it'll just get in the way.' He moved his hand in a steady, intimate rhythm to demonstrate his intentions, and it nearly drove her mad. 'It isn't as if you haven't . . .' He broke off and his face set as he fought for some kind of control. 'Kate, honey, don't torment me.'

But she wasn't. She was just paralytically numb. It wasn't as if she hadn't—*what*? But he didn't seem to realise he had said anything out of place. Did he think she had done this kind of thing before? . . . That she made a habit of it? Was he doing this, not from any affection, but because he thought she was available, and only too willing?

The horror of what he must think of her was suddenly appalling.

CHAPTER SEVEN

'GREG—please—you don't understand . . .' And some note of desperation must have got through, because he was raising his head again, smiling down at her, tracing reassuring circles across her temples.

'It'll be all right—trust me.'

'No, I don't mean . . .' But she wasn't allowed to get further as Greg began gently coaxing again.

Then slowly his face clouded, as if he finally realised what she had been trying to say. 'Just what *do* you mean, Kate? That you haven't . . .' he whispered fiercely. 'That you're a . . .' He looked totally thunderstruck and she could only bite her bottom lip and nod despairingly. 'God in heaven, Kate—what the hell do you think you're up to?' he exploded, pulling away from her as if it was torture. 'I thought—I could have . . . Kate, didn't you have any idea?—coming back in here,' he ranted on, 'wearing that damned nightgown!' Then he groaned, suddenly lost for words, but Kate certainly wasn't. He had the cheek to accuse *her*!

'I'm wearing this nightgown,' she began indignantly, pushing him away and struggling up, 'because I didn't know I'd be sharing my sleeping arrangements with you. And I came back in here, *if* you remember, because we've been taken over by a great herd of seals . . .'

'Come off it, Kate, they're not going to hurt anyone—I was just finding you an excuse, and you know it,' he said savagely, groping for his sweater and pulling it on.

'Are you telling me those great blundering animals out there are harmless?' Her eyes flashed up at him. 'That you tricked me into coming back in here . . .' But something in his expression stopped her going further. A frightening calm had settled over him, and she had seen that controlled anger before.

'It seems we're both good at tricks, Kate.' His voice was icy. 'Yesterday it was your turn—today it appears to be mine. So, okay, you might not know what it's all about—yet—but you're learning fast. Didn't I say I'd teach you the rest? And you'll admit I was right about something else as well.' She raised her chin mutinously and glared, but it didn't bother him. 'I said you'd find a repeat performance most acceptable. Think yourself lucky that even *I* still have a few scruples.' Then he unzipped the tent flap in three vicious, jerky movements.

'Where—where are you going?' Kate was suddenly afraid. Surely he wouldn't just drive away?

'For a swim.' His eyes nearly drove her into the ground. 'And you'd better hope it cools me off. While

I'm gone you can pack up this lot,' and he glanced quickly at the turmoil of bedding. 'We might as well make an extra early start. It's a sure thing neither of us is going to get any more sleep.'

Then he was gone, and Kate rocked back on her heels, breathing out in a long whistle. What a way to get rid of all the tensions that should have been released so beautifully! So Greg had chosen an icy dip. Good luck to him—may he catch pneumonia. But Kate had no such remedy, and therefore no such relief, and it took ages to roll up everything into any kind of order. But with the slow steadying of her nerves came an edgy restlessness. She felt relieved— didn't she?—that nothing had happened. So why did she feel like crying?

But nothing would make her. And when she heard Greg moving around outside again, she scrambled into jeans and a sweater and grabbed her clean underclothes and sponge bag.

'Downstream!' he called out, as she made her way towards the river. Oh, why did he always have to be so right! And she glowered at him as she turned round and headed the other way.

She sat by the water's edge for a long time trying to gather up the courage to strip off and wash in all that cold water. But perhaps she deserved such a penance. Had she really believed those seals were dangerous? Wasn't there the slightest chance that she had been using them as an excuse too? But that was no reason for him to act like that just because I asked for a sweater, thought Kate, pulling this one over her head. But was this what Greg had seen in the early light of dawn? A girl with dark hair in disarray, and the gentle contours of supple breasts and a neat waist. She had sat beside him without thinking, but that nightdress was practically transparent—and if the sun had been coming up ... Kate splashed the cold water over her body and her reflection shattered into a million ripples. But the smile couldn't be shattered, it remained on her lips and lingered awhile as she dressed and brushed her long dark hair. It was exciting to think her body had been able to arouse Greg's passion. It was exciting, but also a little frightening, as was the realisation that she was no longer mistress of her own actions. Greg had been right about her finding his advances most acceptable. And if he hadn't had a few scruples, how long would she have been able to hold off? But she wouldn't have even told him she was a virgin if she thought he cared for her one scrap ... and that was the most frightening thing of all.

Kate wandered back to the camp, suddenly not wanting to get there, not wanting to return to the responsibilities of this trip. And you didn't let any old person make love to you, she reasoned. Not if they had liked you for years, not if you thought they were really quite nice. You only made love with someone you loved—and that was why she hadn't got round to it yet.

'You all right?' Greg was watching her shrewdly,

standing over the stove preparing breakfast.

'What?' Kate blinked. 'Oh yes, fine,' she added nonchalantly. 'I've just got to pack away my sponge bag ...' and she dived back into the tent and found the duffle bag he had lent her yesterday. Of course she didn't love him. What, *Greg Henderson*? No— never in a thousand years!

It wasn't easy to sit with disapproving straightness and keep a haughty profile whenever Greg glanced at her. Not when you were leaping about in a wretched Land Rover that performed more like a bucking bronco. But Kate did her best, and it really was possible to sit there the whole morning without saying a word.

It was a much better day today, the sky stretched away into a pale, duck-egg blue, until it gradually mingled with the distant, hazy moorland. There was only the occasional fluffy white cloud to make things interesting, and of course the wind had come back again. But Kate had tied a scarf, peasant fashion, around her head, so everything was under control.

Even *him*, thanks be praised, and she cast another surreptitious look without moving her head. Yes, you ought to look cross, she thought, carrying your disgusting mind around with you. Imagine thinking I'm always leaping into bed ... And she had been fool enough to imagine, just for a moment, by the way he seemed to care—by the way he had held back until she was ready ... Surely he couldn't have done that without some feeling for her? Or was she just trying to find an excuse for her own behaviour? She bit her lip uncertainly and they bumped and swayed on in silence.

'Are those penguins?' By mid-afternoon animosity was wearing a bit thin. Would they ever reach this Tom fellow? How much longer now? And the sight of three statuesque figures on a bumpy incline had brought forth Kate's excited comment. 'Can we stop just a minute?' she implored. 'Please, I must take a photo,' and grabbing her own camera from the impressive selection in the gadget-bag, she let herself out of the cab.

She approached the penguins cautiously, and in the view-finder they gazed at her with disinterested aloofness, looking like a trio of athletes standing on a podium waiting to collect first, second and third prizes. Kate snapped away, and they really let her get quite close, but as soon as she climbed back into the cab she knew there was something wrong.

Greg's face was all hard angles, only this time he didn't need any gaslight to accentuate them. He started the engine and let out the clutch so fiercely that she was almost shot into the back. Now what was the matter with him? Was he bad-tempered just because they had stopped for five minutes? Huh! Miserable creature. But at least she had those photographs, which would remind her of some of the pleasanter aspects of this island.

The next time they brewed up Greg spread out the map over the bonnet.

'Is it much further?' Kate asked, trying to keep the tiredness out of her voice. It would be fatal to show him how shattered she felt.

He was smoothing out the creases and running a large, bronzed hand over the complicated pattern of colours and squiggles.

'Ten miles, give or take a bit.' He pointed to a cross he had marked on the paper, and Kate wandered over and peered down, pretending to recognise it all.

'Does that mean we reach Tom by nightfall?' she asked, when he had scrutinised their position and began to refold the map. Even that awkward job seemed quite straightforward to him.

'With luck—if we don't hang about here too long,' he added, which was another dig, delivered, this time, with uncharacteristic irritableness.

Kate gulped down the rest of her coffee and began packing up the box again. Greg left her to it and walked around the vehicle, checking the tyres with the toe of his boot. She followed his progress with uncertain eyes. So the end of their journey alone was almost over. She had been out here with him for nearly two days. The figure of Dougal McInnes momentarily drifted into her mind. If she was ever going to discuss the question of the wretched oil, now was going to be the best time to begin.

'Ready?' Greg had climbed into the Land Rover and was staring back at her. There was a strange, fixed look about his face, a sort of caged wariness, that Kate found rather frightening.

He hardly waited for her to slam the door before they were off again and she had to brace herself as they lurched away.

Where could she begin? What on earth would Greg say when she told him the truth? In a minute she would know. Then there would be no more speculation—no more dread. It was all going to be out in the open, and he could rant and rave, go berserk—anything. It wouldn't make any difference, because she had nothing to lose. But it didn't feel like it. It felt like the most awful moment she had ever experienced. What did she usually say at times like these? She racked her brain. But it was useless to imagine Greg Henderson reacting in the same way as her former opponents. Maybe it wouldn't matter much what she said, as long as she said something. And she ran a tongue over her dry lips before proceeding.

'There must be quite a lot of your land that you never actually visit,' she began with a note of fatalism. Now she was committed.

'Visit?' he queried. Trust him to answer with a question.

'I mean, there's so much of it. With nothing here. There'd be no point just travelling around . . .

'You think there's nothing here?' He seemed still caught up in some thoughts or other, as if he wasn't really paying attention. But finally he took one hand off the steering wheel to gesticulate broadly. 'Nothing, Kate? I see plenty of things to interest me.'

'But there's no purpose to any of it. It's just wild moorland . . .'

She could sense he was suddenly alert, and when he spoke again his deep voice was heavy with irony.

'Without purpose?' Today he seemed to be repeating everything she said. Why couldn't he think of some words of his own?

'Not productive, then,' she managed to suggest. But this wasn't getting any easier. Quite the reverse, in fact. Was he deliberately prolonging the agony? Playing cat and mouse? Only this cat was a lion—and hadn't she thought, once before, that she was walking straight into the lion's den? What would happen when retribution came? Kate offered up a silent prayer and waited.

'And its not being productive is important to you?' Now there was nothing hesitant in his manner. He was right beside her mentally as well as physically.

'I would have thought it was important to you,' she said, trying to sound casual.

'Life isn't all balance sheets and statistics, Kate.' She felt him glance for her reaction, but she kept her eyes straight ahead.

'I thought farmers were always hard up,' she announced to the filthy windscreen.

'Do I give that impression?'

'Hardly.' She tried to laugh. 'Of course, I don't know anything about the land. But if it isn't all good grazing—perhaps you could find some other way . . .' She trailed off, but her words seemed to echo around the confined space, then hang, suspended, in front of them. Greg was a long time answering, and she measured the minutes with dread.

'And just what other way would you suggest?'

'There—there must be many things. . . .' She tried to swallow. Greg was slowing down. Not for any obstacles, but because he obviously wasn't paying attention to his driving. 'Maybe . . .' she stumbled.

'Yes? Go on—I'm listening.' And he was. Every nerve in him seemed to be stretched. His hand on the steering wheel clenched and unclenched. His powerful thighs seemed to strain under the constriction of heavy cords. And inside of him, she was aware of a huge spring gradually coiling itself tighter and tighter. 'I'm waiting,' he said sharply, as the truck bumped over a pothole. 'What's the matter, Kate? Run out of ideas?' Then, suddenly, the truck jerked to a halt as he stamped on the brake in fury. He glared down at her, his eyes shining like black ice—and she was suddenly frozen with fear. He knew! He knew everything. He had known all along!

She stared at him in horror. Goodness knows what she must look like. She tried to blink, to break the image of his face creased in anger, of those eyes that wouldn't release her own. Her throat dried completely, and her hammering heart seemed to fill her whole mind.

'You're not even a photographer, are you?' he roared, his coil finally snapping. 'Taking pictures of penguins with an Instamatic—when you've got that fancy array,' he accused, glancing at the gadget-bag at her feet. Then his head shot back and he gave a brief, contemptuous laugh. 'I thought at least that part of your story was true. Even if your magazine was in league with . . .' He broke off, and the corner of his lip curled, showing a glimpse of perfect white teeth in a rugged, tanned face. 'Go on, Kate, confess. Tell me you work for the McInnes crowd—and that you've come out here for no other reason than to get the concession to drill for oil on my land!'

Failure washed over Kate. Failure, wretchedness and desolation. She couldn't move, she couldn't speak—and silence condemned her.

'Right! Get out!'

Her eyes flew open.

'I said—*out*!' Greg's whole presence seemed to fill the cab. It enveloped her, stifled her. Every muscle liquefied and she waited paralytically for the crushing blow. But she couldn't possibly get out. What?— in the middle of nowhere? *Anything* was better than that.

But Greg wasn't standing for any nonsense. 'Out,' he had said, and 'out' he meant, and muttering under his breath he wrenched open the door and marched round the front of the vehicle to Kate's side.

Panic rose swiftly and her eyes suddenly caught sight of the keys still swinging from the ignition. It was just a chance—it might work—and with a desperate effort she scrabbled over to his seat and tried to start the engine. It wouldn't fire. *Damn!* And already it was too late. Greg had seen what she was up to, and the passenger door was nearly swung off its hinges as he stretched inside and grabbed her.

'Oh no, you don't. Leave me, would you—and how far do you think you'd get out here, my girl?' He had her by the arm and was yanking her out on to the rough, stony ground.

Kate fought, kicked and wriggled, but it was like battering against an armoured tank. 'Well, this is it,' she thought, wondering that her brain could still work. 'You're just going to be left—or murdered—or . . .' She tried to think of what her parents would say when they read the headline, 'the body of a young woman . . .'

'You little spitfire!' Greg was holding her from him —shaking her at arm's length. And he was so big and powerful, and there was nothing she could do about it—and she wished she had never heard of this oil and why had they sent her here—and why couldn't he have loved her just a little bit—and he might as well kill her now because there was no future in any of this at all.

'Look at me!' Greg was shouting. 'Kate, listen to me—can't you understand?' He was trying to make her open her eyes and see something. But they were open, yet all she could see was his thunderous rage. He looked ugly—well, almost ugly. And *I've* done it. *I've* caused it, she thought. And that was the worst hurt of all!

'I can't help it—it isn't my fault.' Any old words tumbled out.

'But it would be my fault if I allowed it to happen. Can you imagine the devastation? The oil slicks—

the pollution. No way!' He pushed her from him and she stumbled backwards. 'Not at any price, Kate. Not even to save your head. Life's too precious—this kind of life, I mean. The life down here.' Then he picked up a pebble and hurled it into a puddle with all the pent-up fury of a man almost pushed to the end of his endurance. Then he turned back and looked at her with such loathing that Kate promptly forgot how guilty she had felt just a moment ago.

'There's no need to look at me as if I belong to Murder Incorporated,' she fumed, pulling off the scarf that had fallen over the back of her head in the struggle. Maybe he wasn't going to murder her after all, and relief made her brave. 'There is such a word as progress, you know. You don't seem to mind making use of a bit of it when it suits you.' His brows shot together, but she didn't let him speak. 'Generators for electricity, central heating when the peat fire isn't enough, areoplanes—not exactly backwoods country, is it?'

'If you can't see the difference . . .'

'No, I can't,' she interrupted.

'Then there's little point in my trying to explain . . .' And he might just as well have added, 'to someone as idiotic as you,' because it was obviously on the tip of his tongue. 'I don't know who or what put us all to-gether, Kate,' he began again, and she looked up at him grudgingly, 'but this much of it is mine. In trust, you might say, for the future. And if there *is* going to be a future, we're going to have to be very, very careful, or the only thing we'll be left with is a horrible, horrible mess.'

Involuntarily, her eyes followed his as they swept over the desolate moorland. They both saw two little birds fearlessly playing hopscotch only a few feet from the truck. The wind blew fresh and clean straight from the South Atlantic, sharpening the day, brightening the pale light, bringing a newness with it that Kate hadn't noticed before. She had a momentary vision of oil rigs, drilling and utter pandemonium. To set all that down here would be a crime.

But it wasn't for her to judge. There were plenty of things one had to do without liking it.

'We'd better get a move on.' Greg rubbed the back of his head and looked down at her thoughtfully. Did he know she hadn't given up yet? She lowered her eyes so that he shouldn't see her determination. Maybe there wasn't any future in it at all. So wasn't that a good reason to get exactly what she had come for? She worked for Inpet, didn't she? What about her obligations to them?

She climbed back into the truck and watched with wary eyes as Greg strode around to his side. His face didn't look ugly any more, just sort of fixed in an expression of impenetrable hardness. Right at this moment she had never been more aware of the strength of him. Whether he was making love to her in the early dawn, or bombarding her with the full force of his anger, he did it completely—as complete as the barrier he was now dropping down between

them. 'You're the opposition, therefore I reject you!'
The words were as clear as if he had spoken them
aloud.

Kate wished more than ever for the concealment of
darkness. But from perversity, day lingered and evening crept in slowly. But thankfully shapes in the distance gradually washed into greyness and she realised
she had been staring at the outline of a cottage for
several moments. Had they actually arrived? Was
this dreadful journey nearly over? Going back
wouldn't be half so bad; there would be this Tom
fellow for company.

'Why didn't you tell me the truth?' asked Greg suddenly. They were very close to the house now, and
Kate could see a flickering light shining out into the
gloom. He pulled up next to a wall, almost as if he
didn't want the occupants of the cottage to hear their
arrival. 'Did you really imagine you could fool me?
That you could persuade me to go against my principles?' He was watching her astutely, his anger turning to near amazement that she had actually imagined
such a feat possible.

She remained silent. There was nothing else to do.
Why didn't he drive on? Why didn't he let her get
out? She was tired, cold, absolutely worn out with
everything, and still he kept on at her. And now, as
she watched, she saw the firmness of his face change
to lines of scorn as an idea seemed to occur to him.

'Is that what you were trying to do this morning,
Kate? Were you trying to persuade me? Is that why

London sent a woman?' He gave a harsh laugh. 'And you've been trying to tell me you're civilised up there!' A large hand quickly captured her chin and forced her face upwards.

Kate caught her breath. His eyes were shining with a dangerous message, and she suddenly realised she had never really known this man. On his face were mirrored thoughts she didn't understand; lessons she had never had time to learn. She was strangely aware of the vastness of him, and it wasn't just his physical strength. She glimpsed a vastness of mind; a broad plane of imagination, and a million events, hopes and dreams from the past and in the future, that he would never share with her. It made him so much a stranger, but so unbelievably exciting, and her body responded to the thrill long before his mouth crushed down on hers.

The kiss went on and on; hungrily, demanding, savage and with a touch of bitterness. But Kate didn't care why he was doing it—only that he was. And she didn't want him to stop—ever. It was instinct to respond, to feel the back of his powerful neck straining as she teased her fingers into his hair. She felt rather than heard him gasp, and the she knew she was losing him, he was drawing away—and the pain of it was appalling.

He looked down at her and his eyes were brittle with anger.

'That's right, Kate,' he whispered, every muscle in his face working overtime. 'Don't disappoint me.

Don't give up yet. I want to see just how far you're really prepared to go. I've already shown you there are no half measures on this island. It has to be a one hundred per cent commitment—with no room for manoeuvring.' He ran a cruel finger lightly across her cheek. 'It's a hard life, sweet Kate. Only the fit survive.'

CHAPTER EIGHT

'SHE'S a photographer,' said Greg, when they finally
went into the cottage and he had made the necessary
introductions. The replacement shepherd, as expected, had arrived first. A horse was obviously the
ideal transport on Drake, thought Kate, as the man
nodded towards her, as if he was always seeing young
ladies turn up in the middle of nowhere at the drop of
a hat. But Tom's response was just the opposite. He
looked thunderstruck to see Kate's slim figure hovering uncertainly behind Greg. He looked thunderstruck—and absolutely delighted—and she tried to
match his cheerful smile.

But nothing was working. Not her mind—not her
usual reflexes. She knew she was here at last, and
there was a flickering oil lamp on the bare wooden
table. She knew that Greg and the old fellow were
sitting discussing the situation, and she was perched
beside an ancient settee, trying to make conversation
with a cheerful-looking man with tired blue eyes. And
thank heavens he didn't seem to notice she was talking in monosyllables.

'And your magazine is doing a story about us ...
And you've come all this way by yourself—alone ...
And Mr Henderson let you come out here ...' The
odd 'yes' or 'no' seemed to suffice, but Kate wasn't
really concentrating. Greg's kiss was still fresh on her
lips, her heart still dancing, and she found herself paying more attention to the decisions and pronounce-
ments being made on the other side of the room.

The shepherd was nodding, tapping out his pipe
and refilling it, and he was watching Greg with a kind
of canny wariness. Kate suddenly realised that Greg
would have been a child when this man first began
dealing with sheep, yet he showed no sign of indul-
gence. Greg Henderson commanded respect—and he
received it.

But respect wasn't the only feeling Greg Henderson
had commanded that night. Kate's eyes flickered
around them all, seeing the men talking quietly; the
dogs curled in a heap, fire and lamplight softening the
austerity, and she realised nobody would know that
ten minutes ago Greg had been kissing her quite ruth-
lessly. And nobody would ever know, either, that she
had fallen in love with him so completely. She was as
sure of it as she was sure of her own name. And it
was frightening, and all quite hopeless, but it also
gave her a kind of strength. No one could stop her
feeling proud of him. The way he organised everything, or for being the sort of man he was, with the
ideals he held. But vulnerability ran hand in hand
with strength, and Kate knew she would have to

learn the trick of juggling them together.

'Have you come to play your ministering angel act, as well?' Tom asked, and she blinked a couple of times and tried to concentrate.

'I'll see what I can manage,' she said, smiling into eyes that for a second had flickered nervously.

When Greg finally came over and looked at Tom's injuries, Kate moved away, but not before she had glimpsed a bruised, swollen and obviously very painful leg. Poor Tom; it was little wonder he showed no enthusiasm for the journey back to Sealbank.

After supper there was really nothing to do but go to bed. Conversation wasn't exactly riveting and even if she had felt up to it—the light wasn't good enough to read by. It was Greg who offered to show her Tom's room.

'But I can't take his bed,' she began to protest.

'He's hardly in a position to get up there,' said Greg, sorting out the bedding they had brought in from the truck.

Kate bit the insides of her cheek, clutched the paraphernalia he tossed her way, and silently followed him. There were some things you just didn't say in company!

The stairs were narrow, dark, bare-boarded and noisy. There was one door at the top and Greg pushed it open. Inside, the ceiling swooped low and moonlight shone through a tiny window. There was a saggy bed with brass ends and a thick patchwork quilt.

'If you put your sleeping bag on top we won't have

to worry about the sheets. I'll get you a light. Is there anything else?' Kate shook her head, but of course he wasn't looking her way. 'Mmm?' he said impatiently, and this time she managed to answer in a tiny voice.

But there was such a lot she really wanted. Not just him coming and going and bringing back an oil lamp which filled the tiny room under the roof with a rough kind of comfort. If only he wouldn't be so brusque, if he would kiss her goodnight, even just a peck, to show some kindness. But of course, he didn't, not even with the lamp flickering around the place making it all look so cosy.

'It may not be quite what you've been used to,' Greg turned towards her at last, waving a hand dispassionately. 'But I think you'll be comfortable for one night.' She noticed a slight catch in his voice as he finished speaking. The lamp hissed and popped, but they just stared at each other, as jerky shadows danced on the wall next to them. Kate felt hot, suffocated, the blood throbbed in her temples and gradually she saw the answering response of Greg's own desire. Tension touched his cheek, flared his nostrils and sent life pulsating out of him in shallow, jerky movements. In a minute Kate knew she was going to fade away. Never, ever, had she wanted anyone so much in all her life.

'Gets to you, Kate, doesn't it?' The shattered silence brought no relief. 'It's the island, you see. Our *uncivilised* island. The days are hard, and we don't have time for many fancy ideas. But at the end of a day,'

he broke off, taking a pace nearer, and ran wild eyes
over her weary figure. 'At the end of a day all a man
needs is a warm meal,' he laughed harshly, 'and a
warm bed. But it takes a special sort of person to fill
it, Kate. Did you know that? Do you even know what
I'm trying to say?' Before she realised what was happening he had crossed the narrow gap between them
and two powerful hands grasped her arms viciously.
'We don't have room for career girls down here. A
woman has to be a warm, loving homemaker.' Con-
flict threatened to tear him apart. 'And you're not
that, Kate, are you?'

'I never said I was . . .' She tried to break away.

'No, you didn't.' He seemed to enjoy her struggles.
'So what does that make you—hmm? The other sort
of woman? The tempting, provocative, persuading
kind of woman?' Passion seemed to tangle inside him,
a need to punish her conflicting with desire. He
wanted her yet he hated her. Oh yes, she knew exactly how he felt.

'I think you'd better leave,' she heard herself say.
'They'll be wondering downstairs. . . .'

'They won't be wondering,' Greg interrupted.
'They'll know precisely what I'm doing—what I
should have done before. You're right, Kate: you
never tried to be anything but a persuader. Why
shouldn't I take advantage of it? What difference can
it make?'

'The difference is respect,' she said, breaking free
at last.

'Respect,' he repeated harshly. 'Yours?'

'Hardly.' She saw his immediate anger and hurried on, 'I mean the men downstairs. What about their respect?'

'You know little about men,' he said, advancing again, and Kate backed off. 'What respect do you think they'll have if I don't stay up here for the night? And let's see if you have any respect for this . . .'

Instinct warned her too late. Suddenly she was pulled against Greg's chest, then swung off her feet and tumbled unceremoniously on to the bed. His fingers searched for the fastening of her jeans and she wriggled and squirmed, but he only laughed, and the old bed groaned in sympathy.

'How dare you! I'll scream. . . .'

'Go ahead.' The button came undone. 'They've got more sense than to interfere.' The zip was sticking, thank heaven, and she brought her knee upwards, but he pinned it back down without effort. 'That's right, Kate, fight me. Show me how much you think you hate me.' The metal teeth gave way a couple of inches. 'And then we'll see if I can get your respect as a lover,' he taunted. 'I'm good, Kate. Some say very good.' A warm, firm hand slid over her stomach and she flinched. 'Do you want to find out just how good I really am?'

'I wouldn't want you if you were the last man on this earth . . .'

But she was stopped from elaborating as Greg began kissing her. Slowly and firmly his mouth worked on hers, until she wasn't flinching any more, in fact she had stopped fighting altogether, and warm, pulsating tremors seemed to flow from his body into her own.

'And you say you don't want me.' Greg's voice was unfathomable, and Kate could have wept for showing her feelings so easily.

'But then I'm bound to, aren't I?' she managed to say in little more than a whisper. 'You're good at it—you admitted it yourself—but it's only physical reaction.' Now he was really listening to her, his body heavy against her own. 'But there's no feeling,' Kate continued, surprising even herself, 'no love. And that's what counts in my book. Without it,' she made a helpless little gesture and blinked, hoping her tears wouldn't be seen, 'without it we're no better than animals.'

He gazed down at her for a long moment, a big, dark man towering over her in the shadowy room. 'You should have thought of that earlier.' His voice sounded brittle. 'I said if you came it would be by my rules—and that's what I meant.' One hand stretched across her waist and pinned her down helplessly. 'Well, tonight you can sleep alone, Kate, because *I* allow it. You can thank me for it, if you like, during the hours you stay awake wondering how it's going to be when I decide you *don't* sleep alone. And don't say over your dead body—or remind me of my scruples,' he went on when she tried to say something, 'because don't imagine I extend my scruples to such devious members of the opposition. We may have some unfinished business, my sweet Kate, but it's for when *I* decide to finish it.' Then, with a disdainful thrust, he heaved himself off her and abruptly left the room. What had he said earlier? Only the fit survive.

Oh, I'll survive somehow, afterwards, Kate thought, and much later she turned over in the old bed to the accompaniment of squeaky springs. Downstairs the low murmuring of the three men had finally subsided. All was quiet, night had stilled the restless wind, yet it hadn't performed similarly on Kate's heart.

Greg's kiss out in the truck tonight had been a revelation. And the time he had spent up here with her had only accentuated the longing for him, and the misery of knowing she meant absolutely nothing at all to him.

Had she really loved him from the beginning? That day he had burst through the office door at the airport; all dark, domineering and wildly attractive. Or was it later, when she had seen him in the hotel lounge with Laura? Then his restlessness had been covered by a mantle of quiet sophistication—just as the wind blew remorselessly all day, only to be silent at night. How alike they were, the island and this man.

And had everything she had said, or thought, only been a deception? All the *trying* to hate him, because he stood in the way of her making a success of this assignment. Could she really stack the principles of her job against personal feelings for another human being? Never mind the broader aspects of the problem; pollution versus protection. That was happening everywhere and Kate knew she couldn't take on the responsibilities for the whole world. But this wasn't the whole world, it was just one small island. But it was Greg's world, and it wouldn't have mattered if it was the moon or Outer Mongolia—he loved it, and that was what mattered most of all.

But, whatever she thought, and however she felt, he would never love her simply because he thought she didn't understand. Understand? Huh! But didn't he understand people in London had faith in her? Didn't they have the right to expect her loyalty? And Kate knew she could only be loyal to one person at a time.

Greg's sun-bronzed, magnetic, wide-awake face hovered in her imagination. If only he had loved her it wouldn't have mattered that she worked for the opposition. They could have sorted it out. She could have explained to Dougal. But what she was on the outside mattered more to Greg than who she was on the inside. Didn't he know it was the inside person who mattered most of all? But maybe he just didn't want to see.

Oh, why did everything have to be so complicated? She bounced over to her other side and winced at the noise the bed made. Could they hear?—the three men downstairs, and thinking of them reminded her of Tom again and the journey which would be torture for him.

In the stillness outside she heard a horse whinny and stamp its foot, and the answering response from one of the dogs. Then all was peaceful again. Instinctively she realised it would be as well to make the most of this brief respite. Tomorrow they would be off again. Tom might have his problems, but she wondered just what kind of torture Greg Henderson would have in store for her.

'I get the impression you and the governor are a bit . . .' Tom broke off, peering at her from the back of the truck and wincing slightly as he attempted to wriggle into a more comfortable position. They were halfway through the following morning, Greg was checking a rattle that had developed under the bonnet and Kate had made their usual coffee restorative. At Tom's comment she glanced quickly through the windscreen, but Greg hadn't heard, he was still engrossed in his repairs.

Now she looked back at Tom. 'I have had better trips,' she admitted at last.

'He must want his head read.' And this time sympathy was replaced by open admiration.

Kate returned his smile, noticing for the first time, that really he was quite a nice looking fellow. A bit of an adventurer, she guessed. Tough, wiry—and obviously a loner. Wouldn't it take a special sort of person to be prepared to stay out here in the wilds with only two dogs for company? Her eyes lowered to Tom's hand, automatically fondling a black and white shaggy head that was nestling against him. Yes, the dogs would be a comfort—but he would need a strength of his own to survive out here.

Suddenly Tom wasn't quite the cheeky young shepherd she had barely thought about. He was very real, and Kate wished she could get to know him better.

'I'm surprised he flew you out here if he's so anti,' Tom began again, and Kate swivelled round in her seat to face him.

'He didn't exactly offer to bring me out to Sealbank,' she admitted, and, as there was no point in continuing with the lie, she told him about the radio broadcast—and about tricking Greg into bringing her —and then she told him who she really was.

Tom let out his breath in a low, incredulous whistle. 'And he's only just found out?'

Kate nodded. 'Yesterday afternoon; not long before we reached your place. But that's why I came,' she added hastily. 'I had to tell him—to try and explain.' She shrugged hopelessly. 'And this trip seemed the best way of getting his undivided attention.'

'I should think you got that all right,' Tom muttered. 'Right mad, was he?'

Kate nodded once more and closed her eyes for a moment, remembering just how mad Greg had been.

'And you work for that crazy Scotsman?' said Tom, shaking his head in bewilderment.

'Dougal isn't crazy,' Kate laughed.

'He was by the time our governor had finished with him. I was there—back at Sealbank,' Tom explained. 'McInnes came, and a couple of other chappies— engineers, I suppose.' He shook his head briefly. 'I don't really know what happened. But there was an awful fuss. They'd chartered one of his planes, you see. I think the office thought they wanted it for another survey. But they came out to see us, although they didn't stay long,' Tom added, and his mischievous grin painted a vivid picture of Greg Henderson's fiery temper. 'They didn't come back again, either,' he concluded, and there was something so comical about the way he said it that Kate couldn't help laughing.

'I know I shouldn't,' she groped for a hanky and wiped her eyes, and one of Tom's dogs watched her with mounting suspicion. 'It's just that I know Dougal,' she muttered helplessly, 'and he's so—so— bombastic—and there were three of them. . . .' And then her laughter died and suddenly they were looking at each other quite seriously.

'You've sure picked yourself some opponent,' observed Tom, and before Kate could reply the bonnet crashed down. Apparently the man under discussion had finished his handiwork.

Greg walked round the truck and dumped the tool box in the back, then began wiping his hands on an oily rag. Dark, suspicious eyes glanced from Tom to Kate, where they lingered awhile and brought forth

a guilty flush to her cheeks. Silence stretched out into
the wilderness. A chilly wind ruffled Greg's hair and
flapped at the corner of his parka. It was as if he was
aware of every word that had been spoken. Kate saw
his strong, usually readable features, for once enig-
matic. She shifted uneasily in her seat and glanced
quickly at Tom for support. But the pale blue eyes
flickered away from her self-consciously.

When she looked back at Greg, who was still leaning against the tailboard, she saw a taunting twist to
his lips, and the eyebrow with the quirk at the end was
raised in cruel delight. 'You see,' came his silent response, 'you won't get any help from that quarter.'
There was no need for actual words—and he knew
it.

As the day wore on it became obvious that Tom
wouldn't be able to come to Kate's rescue even if he
had wanted to. Their chirpy passenger fell silent
around mid-afternoon, and by the time Greg was de-
ciding on a decent site for the night, Tom appeared to
be in a good deal of pain.

'He's feverish as well,' Greg reported later, having
made him as comfortable in the Land Rover as their
slender means would allow. 'I've given him another
jab, he's pretty restless, let's hope it quietens him
down,' he added, watching Kate struggle with billy
cans and a gas jet that kept going out. 'I'll see to that.'
His exasperation was evident, and she was about to
retort, when he added. 'You go and sit with Tom,'
which sounded like an excuse to rescue the supper,

but when she climbed up beside the young shepherd he really did look in need of a hand to cling to.

They had their meal in relays, and when Greg had finished his Kate heard him stroll across to the truck.

'How is he?' he whispered, pulling aside the canvas back-flap and nodding towards their patient.

'He comes and goes a bit,' she said quietly, edging her way past the sleeping boy. 'I've given him a drink, just a drop of water.'

'Do you want to stretch your legs?' She could sense his quick appraisal. It seemed concern for Tom had brought a temporary respite to the hostilities. 'I've made some coffee,' he said after a moment. 'I should think Tom will be all right for a little while now.'

Kate let herself be helped to the ground. It was dark outside, and she saw a million brilliant stars pinpointing the inky sky of other worlds. She sighed, wishing she could discover similar glimpses of light down here in this world.

Greg's camp looked cosy, the tent illuminated by a soft light making it almost transparent. The smell of coffee was good; she saw two steaming mugs next to the stove.

'Sit down.'

She shook her head. 'I've been cooped up long enough,' she said, taking the drink and shuffling around selfconsciously. There was only one place to sit—in there—and nothing was going to get her inside that tent with Greg Henderson tonight. Funny! She took a sip of the strong brew to hide a whimsical smile. What had she said all along? You only made love with someone you loved. But what if they didn't love you? Ah! That was a good question and she was simply too worn out even to try and think of an answer.

'Do you think Tom has really broken his leg?' She had wandered out of the circle of light and now she glanced back over her shoulder and was surprised to see Greg's hunky silhouette steadily regarding her. She looked away quickly, kicked a pebble and had another sip of coffee before he replied.

'It'll probably take an X-ray to tell that.' He spoke the words as if he was giving them only half his attention. What was really on his mind? Kate didn't want to think about it.

'He seems pretty poorly tonight. Worse than last night. Do you think it's because of the journey?'

She could sense Greg's shrug. 'Could be.' Then there was silence again.

'I don't suppose there's any stew left.'

'No.'

'Shall I wash up?'

'I've done it.'

She heard him lay the mug on a flat stone. Had he finished his coffee already? Now what would happen? Her mind went numb until she heard the sound of more coffee being poured from the pot. Relief— momentarily, at least. If only Tom would call out. If only she wasn't here, feeling so desperately alone, surrounded by such vast areas of nothing.

She wandered even further away, pretending to look up at the sky with interest. The stars looked different somehow. But of course they would, wouldn't they? This was the Southern Hemisphere. Didn't they have a different set down here?

'It's a good night for flying.' She hadn't heard him walk up behind, the sudden sensation was agony. 'It's just right,' he was saying, looking up as she had been, and now she followed his gaze into the sky again. 'There's no moon tonight,' he went on. 'And if you're up there in the cockpit the stars seem to hang all around you. It's beautiful, Kate. Magical—so peaceful.'

There was a husky inflection in his rich voice that sent her heart racing. He's going to kiss me, she thought in amazement. Maybe he does care . . .

But hope was shortlived. Greg suddenly looked down at the mug in his hand, glanced quickly at Kate, then slowly, with almost tangible strength, pulled himself beyond the realm of such fantasy.

'I've made up your bed.' His voice was harsh once more. 'I'll sleep in the truck with Tom—I don't think he ought to be left tonight.' His words disappeared far out into the night. They were lost for ever—as lost as Kate felt. Lost and terribly alone.

The sleeping-bag was warm; he had left her an extra sweater and a pair of thick-knit socks to pull up to her knees. But the tent was lonely tonight, and Kate had to admit that maybe retribution would have been sweeter than this.

The lion's den. Wasn't that how she had thought of Sealbank when she had first contemplated coming out here? But by late afternoon the following day, Kate realised she would never feel more thankful to see the outline of the white brick house, nestling in its hollow as it looked out to sea. Everyone in the truck had fallen silent hours ago. Tiredness gripped even the fittest of them, while Tom looked strained and almost grey with fatigue.

Their journey had gone without further hitch, helped along by the weather which had been kind to them—kind for Drake Island at any rate. The wind had stirred high cloud into a kaleidoscope of sunlight and shadow all day, and it had kept the rain at bay. But now, as evening crept nearer, the wind was dropping and heavier clouds obscured the top of Greg's mountain. Kate didn't realise the significance of this until she was helping to unload Tom.

'No chance of getting you to that hospital bed tonight, old son,' Greg said, philosophically accepting the vagaries of weather conditions. So he carried him straight upstairs and didn't come down for ages, leaving Kate to begin all the unloading. She had quite a pile on the kitchen table when he eventually came into the room.

'Tom's asleep.' The burnished glow of dark eyes swept over her. 'I'm going to radio Francistown.' He strolled across the room and glanced up at the mountain. 'I'll tell them I'll bring Tom in tomorrow if that lot clears up.' Then he turned from the window and leant back against the sink. Kate could feel his eyes following her every move as she stacked the tins of food they hadn't used on to the dresser. If only he would go and collect the dogs, or go and radio, anything to get him out of this kitchen before she started screaming.

Calm yourself, Kate Lawrence. She wound a strand of hair behind her ear and cast him a surreptitious look under her lashes. He was still doing it—still leaning against the sink, hands thrust into deep trouser pockets, ankles crossed, chin almost resting on his chest, like a large animal silently watching its prey before the attack.

Well, he wasn't going to catch her. Kate tossed her head defiantly and began rummaging in another box. This one had all the cooking gear in it. She sighed. They really ought to have a thorough clean. . . .

'Leave it.' The sudden words startled her. 'I said I was going to radio Francistown, but before I do I want a few words with you.' His voice was heavy with meaning and Kate's courage sank. 'If you can spare me five minutes,' he said formally, crossing the room and holding open the door for her. And when she looked at him uncertainly, he added, 'My study, I think. That's where I usually conduct my business.'

CHAPTER NINE

'WE'VE come a long way, Kate, these past few days.' Greg was rocking back in the chair behind his desk, his eyes steadily regarding her. Under such scrutiny Kate shifted uncomfortably on the only other seat in the room. It was an ancient oak carver, and its back was digging into her. Greg Henderson could certainly pick his instruments of torture!

'It's been a long ride, if that's what you mean,' she said quietly. There was something behind all this, even if, for the moment, the reason escaped her. She looked down at her crumpled jeans and wanted nothing more than to get into a hot bath and soak. But she wasn't being given the opportunity. Greg looked as if he was installed for the duration. Her eyes flickered unconsciously to the silver-edged frame turned towards him. How different we must look, she thought suddenly, one cool blonde and one scruffy brunette. But I wonder how the sophisticated Laura would look if she had just been rescuing shepherds? Probably still cool and blonde. Her sort always did.

'I wasn't only referring to our journey.' Greg's

voice pulled back her attention. 'But you've seen a lot, more than most.' He seemed to hesitate slightly before continuing, 'I was wondering just how important your job is to you.'

Kate was instantly alert, somehow pushing away tiredness. 'It's very important,' she began carefully.

'And the success of your—shall we call it—mission is important too?'

'The one goes with the other.' But surely he realised that. Kate tried not to frown or appear as confused as she felt.

He was looking down at his desk, fiddling with a pencil, but now his eyes slowly raised again to gaze at her intently.

'It's just that you really know what it's like down here,' he went on. 'It's a good life—Jean can tell you that.' And his words recalled the evening they had spent with his manager. How long ago it all seemed, thought Kate. And just think of the mistakes and misjudgments I've made since then. And wasn't falling in love with Greg turning out to be the biggest mistake of all?

'I don't quite know where all this is getting us,' she said, slipping on her professional hat; for a second trying to be the confident young lady Big John would have expected. But Greg's lips twisted wryly; he appeared to have little difficulty seeing through her mask.

'Then I shall tell you where all this is getting us. I am suggesting to you, or maybe I should say—offer-

ing you—a way out of all your problems.' He paused
momentarily as she gasped, then his eyes veiled over
as he added. 'But of course, at my price, on my terms
—as I've said all along.'

There was something in the tone of his voice that
made her heart dance about crazily. Almost as if
amusement wasn't far beneath the surface. He wasn't
talking about the usual deal, she was certain. Could
he be . . .? She held his fixed stare in growing astonishment.

'I see you're beginning to understand.' He sat with
only the desk between them, yet it was as much a
barrier as a six-foot wall. She could see him, but it
wasn't him. He was holding everything back. The
only part of him that seemed alive were those two
dark eyes, and if they were meant to portray his soul
it looked a cold and bleak place to be. 'And does the
idea appeal to you, Kate? Do you think you could
live down here on Drake? Or perhaps I should say out
here at Sealbank, because this is a vastly different
place from Francistown. I can't offer you . . .'

Kate didn't wait to find out what. 'And that's the
price for the concession?' she interrupted. 'You
think Inpet are going to give me a few months off so
that I can stay out here . . .'

He smiled thoughtfully. 'I was imagining something of a longer duration than a few months. Maybe
I'm not explaining very well . . .'

'You're right there.' This was getting worse every
moment. How she would have longed to hear the

words spoken in other circumstances. But like this, with no talk of affection, let alone love. 'And there's no need to explain anything more—I understand quite perfectly. You might run things round here but you don't run me. Now or ever,' she added with definite finality.

'I wasn't suggesting we begin our arrangement— as of this moment,' Greg replied at last, just when she was beginning to wonder how he had managed to remain silent for so long. 'A thing like that takes time . . .'

'*Time!*' Kate tossed at him. 'It takes time, does it?' She didn't know why, but something made her look down at Laura's photograph. 'And how much time did you give her? Or is she just reserved for the city lights? Government House receptions and cosy, candlelit dinners? Wouldn't she object if you had me tucked away? Or is that how you do things down here? Oh yes, you told me once.' She laughed harshly. 'I remember. You said a man needs to come home to a warm meal and a warm bed. Well, the kitchen's that way,' she said, pointing behind her, 'and you can find someone else to warm your bed. Remember me telling you that there has to be love for that kind of thing?' Love on both sides, she nearly added, but stopped herself just in time. 'We don't need your oil that much, Mr Henderson. In fact, I'm even surprised you considered making your proposition at all. Surely your land comes before any personal needs you might have—or that *I* might be able to fulfil. I suggest you find yourself someone else—and we'll find another place to put our rig. Okay?'

'Okay!' He nodded imperceptibly, and laid weary hands on his desk before heaving himself upright. 'You have made your point most succinctly, Miss Lawrence.' She rose as he did and they stared at each other across the mahogany desk. 'I'll radio Francistown and tell them I'm bringing in Tom tomorrow. And shall I tell them I have another passenger?' The eyebrow with the quirk rose fractionally. 'Shall I tell them the photographer has completed her mission—and wants to be returned to *her* kind of civilisation?'

Cold desolation wrung at Kate's heart. 'That might be the best thing all round,' she managed to whisper.

His face remained a mask, only the long muscles down each cheek moved imperceptibly, and she recognised a man who disliked losing even the smallest battle.

They stood facing each other a long time, the quietness punctuated by the measured tick of the grandfather clock out in the hall. The house seemed suddenly hushed. No dogs barked; the wind was still again, then Greg's voice finally broke the silence.

'I'm sure you're right,' he said, in a heavy tone. 'I'll fly you back tomorrow. As you said, that might be the best thing all round.'

The sound of Greg's voice delivering those cold, final words continually haunted Kate during the next three days. She moved back to the Bryants' hotel, visited Tom a couple of times at the cottage hospital, and tried to see Dougal. But he was always out on one of the rigs with the engineer who had flown in with her.

Funny, she hadn't given them any thought during the time she had been out at Sealbank. Normally she would have been caught up with Dougal's problems and frantic phone calls. But all his troubles, much less those back in London, seemed to belong to another world. Some time during the past week she had begun to see things through Greg's eyes. She wasn't quite sure when it started. Was it on the outward trip to fetch Tom? That time Greg had hauled her out of the truck and ranted and raved about the Island? Or had it been earlier, that evening with Jean and Ralph? Only then she had thought it was their contentment she had recognised. But had it been a glimpse of what could have been her own? Some hopes!

She moved restlessly around her bedroom trying to decide what to wear. This evening was just about all she needed. Wasn't it bad enough having to hang about here for the weekly flight out? Why did the Governor have to throw one of his functions now of all times?

'But he can't want to invite me,' Kate had said, returning yesterday from one of her abortive attempts to see Dougal. 'The Governor doesn't know me—I'm not important . . .'

'It's quite the normal thing, really,' Mrs Bryant had told her, having watched her open the invitation and scarcely glance at it. 'He always invites any visitor to whatever's going on. And it's nice to have a fresh face among the usual crowd.'

Usual crowd! Kate wondered, remembering the conversation as she shook out her long pink evening dress and laid it across the bed. Would Greg be one of the usual crowd? Greg with Laura? She would soon find out now.

As Government Houses went, Kate guessed, the residence on Drake Island could quite kindly be termed 'unpretentious'. It was hardly bigger than Greg's house at Sealbank, although more formal of course, and it seemed a ballroom extension had been added at some time, along with an adjoining conservatory.

A car had been sent; it was V.I.P. treatment all the way. Friendly faces greeted her; the Governor turned out to be the sweet little man with whiskers, and soon she was propelled into the throng with questions raining from all sides. But her mind was only half on the conversation. A feeling of unreality began to waft over her. Would Greg arrive or wouldn't he? That seemed to be the only problem filling her mind.

It was funny really, feeling so unsure of herself; wondering if maybe he was somewhere else in the house with Laura; thinking that she would have to see him before she knew he was there. But it was instinct. One minute the room was simply filled with chattering people—and the next moment he was one of them. He came in from somewhere behind her. Was a cool blonde draped on his arm? It was agony not to turn round and look.

'Good evening, Kate.'

She breathed again. He was alone. And she managed a smile as someone handed him a drink and drew him aside. But the interruption gave her a few moments to get over the shock of seeing him. This wasn't the tough sheep farmer who had driven a mud-spattered truck for four solid days. This was the suave, man-of-the-world type Greg, in superb dinner suit and brilliant white evening shirt. She would have traded eternity for one chance of melting into his arms.

Then, from the far side of the room, came another voice she recognised, and through the crush she saw the burly outline of Dougal McInnes. That was all she needed. It looked as if it was going to turn into one of *those* nights.

Somehow their group split up; Greg had been enticed away, so that when she drifted on, she was alone, and seeing his chance, Dougal McInnes pounced.

Kate blinked wearily and tried to meet International Petroleum's representative with something like a smile.

'I hear you've been busy,' she said, trying to disguise soft-soap with concern. 'How is it going out on the rig? Have you much more to do?'

Dougal McInnes was unable to resist talking about his troubles, and the comment that he appeared to have ready was momentarily thrust aside. Yes, the work had been completed, he told her, but only just in time.

Things were always a rush, but why 'just in time'? In time for what? So Kate asked.

'They've got trouble over on the mainland now,' Dougal muttered in annoyance, and Kate realised he was talking about their field in Tierra del Fuego, that wild, desolate land above Cape Horn. 'Our engineer,' Dougal nodded towards the man through the crowd, 'flies out tomorrow—regardless. Never mind if we've finished with his services.' His dark, heavy features flushed angrily and Kate was quick to soothe, until the first part of his comment struck home.

'You say he's flying out tomorrow?' she queried, taking a long-stemmed glass from a waiter who hovered nearby. 'But surely there isn't another flight for a couple of days,' she queried, making rapid calculations as she sipped the bubbly liquid. Champagne —yuck! Still, they said the first glass was the worst, after that you hardly noticed.

'We're chartering a private jet from the mainland,' Dougal informed her casually, such exploits quite normal in his business. 'This isn't bad, is it?'

Kate took another sip. 'No.' She frowned, her mind racing as possibilities presented themselves. If International Petroleum had a flight out tomorrow why shouldn't she be on it? Panic threatened to overwhelm her. More champagne—another sip. Keep calm. Think. She was full of instructions to herself.

What was the alternative? Stay here until Friday in close proximity with Greg in the hope that ... Forget it. No chance in his direction. So why not escape and finish this whole wretched business immediately? She put the question delicately to Dougal.

'You want to leave?' he began abruptly, then his astonishment changed to reluctant admiration. 'You mean you've done it? Good lord, girl, I never thought you would—that's a relief.' His words came quickly, like an excited child, and his heavy-jowled, usually bad-tempered face took on the guise of a benevolent bulldog. But not for long.

'I'm afraid it isn't quite like that,' whispered Kate, looking down at her half-empty glass. 'He hasn't signed—I—I couldn't persuade him.'

In such temperate surroundings Dougal, unable to explode, turned a faint, apoplectic puce.

'And you want out already! Typical!' At least he managed to control the string of expletives Kate guessed had sprung to his lips. 'I told them you didn't have a hope in hell. If *I* couldn't get the concession, how the devil did they expect you to? Bloody waste of time all round. Made us look right fools!'

'I don't think so,' Kate said hastily. 'Mr Henderson always speaks of me as a photographer. I don't think he'll say anything about ...' but she wasn't allowed to finish.

'Bit late for him to start thinking of our feelings.' Or was it *my* feelings? she wondered, then quickly rejected the idea as Dougal continued: 'You've tried everything, I take it?'

'Yes! Practically.' Kate looked warily at her colleague, not wanting him to jump to the wrong conclusion too quickly.

'Have you any idea just how much it cost to send you out here?' Dougal continued. He was in command of himself now, and perhaps because she, too, had failed, he could afford to gloat. 'Have you added up the price of your ticket—the hotel—your expenses . . .?'

'I regret as much as anyone——' Kate began, trying not to lose her temper, but Dougal interrupted in a fierce whisper.

'Equality! Isn't that what you think you have? Doing a man's job, yet wanting to keep your prissy, feminine ideals. That's why you'll never be equal—never totally succeed. In this game you have to forget your scruples.'

Kate blinked. Someone else had talked of scruples. Oh yes, Greg. But his hadn't lasted long either. How easily she was always recalling that dreadful interview in his study. Supposing she hadn't been so hasty —perhaps asked for time to think it over. Then maybe she would be staying here instead of making arrangements to leave. But there would be no going back now. Too many words had been spoken—she felt cold inside. The sooner she could get away from this island the sooner she could return to relative peace of mind.

'I'll leave you to arrange my seat on the plane,' she said simply. 'I'm sure there won't be any objections. If there are,' she shrugged, 'I can always telephone London.' That was a threat, and recognised as such. Dougal didn't like it, but there was nothing he could do.

'Certainly you can accompany my engineer, Miss Lawrence.' And louder for the benefit of those around, 'But I'm surprised you're leaving so soon. I hope your —er—editors in London will think your visit worth while after sending you all the way down here!'

Wretched man! What right had he to suggest . . . Kate patrolled the deserted conservatory, into which she had escaped, before her temper had overcome her and she had slapped his face. Not exactly the type of behaviour suited to Government House. Kate chuckled, in spite of herself, then paused before a splendid oleander whose pale pink blossoms nearly touched the glass-panelled roof. The exotic flowers were geographically out of place, yet the protective glass held them in safe keeping, as Greg held his land in safe keeping, she suddenly thought. If it wasn't for his protection part of Sealbank could be in ruins. A devastation complete as surely as if this glass should shatter and the vicious, Antarctic wind tear its merciless way through these delicate petals.

And yet, in spite of that, even as she gazed at such gentle beauty, she found herself feeling guilty at failing so miserably. Money! The cost of her trip. Dougal's words spun round until, unconsciously, she was groping in her evening bag for her small diary with its pencil tucked down the spine.

There was a circular seat around a gigantic evergreen and she perched on the white slats, making a quick list of figures. Maybe it was guesswork, but the total result was alarming and she stared down at the seemingly endless row of noughts. Had it cost that much? Was anybody's pride worth such a price? Dougal had failed—had Big John expected her to go that far?

It would mean staying here, giving up her job. But those were two decisions she had made during those unfathomable moments when she had begun to love Greg. He didn't love her—but did it matter? Couldn't she be the one to give—to the man she loved, after all? Did there really have to be love on both sides? Maybe if she stayed long enough he would grow to love her too. She looked down at the diary again. Were there that many noughts? So much money— success or failure depending on ... Kate drew a deep breath. Maybe it was almost her duty to stay down here with Greg.

Such an idea needed fortification, and she returned to the ballroom and waylaid the nearest waiter. She gulped half a glass of champagne with as much enthusiasm as if it was castor oil.

They were right—that hadn't been half as bad as the first glass, and a rosy glow wafted into her cheeks. This Greg Henderson fellow would be a walk-over.

She felt herself smiling. It was going to be all right. She *could* go through with it ... And then she saw them; Greg and the cool, beautiful Laura dancing together intimately in the midst of the twirling throng.

CHAPTER TEN

THE music was finishing. Greg and Laura were coming towards her. There was nowhere for Kate to run.

'You haven't met.' The usual comment as he introduced a petite brunette draped in pink silk to a vision of silver chiffon and platinum curls. Laura shimmered beside her dark companion. How they complemented each other, thought Kate. She was like porcelain, so very fragile. She would bring out the tenderest instincts in any man.

'Greg's been telling me all about you, haven't you, darling?' Laura purred, displaying a fine alabaster profile as she gazed up at him.

Kate's dignity was ruffled and he did nothing to soothe it.

'I endeavour to keep you entertained, Laura,' he said quietly, and she rounded wicked eyes at him in silent response.

Kate wished one of the chandeliers would fall on them both. She glanced upwards—but nothing happened.

'I think you're very brave to go gallivanting all

over the place with our Greg,' Laura went on, in a tone that implied *imbecilic* might be a better description. Her luminous eyes swept over Kate. 'I certainly wouldn't camp out in the wilds—Greg said you were practically overrun with seals at one stage.' She visibly shuddered at the idea. And so did Kate. Was that all he had said?

'It was in a good cause,' she said stiffly, then glancing up at Greg, 'I saw Tom at the hospital this afternoon. He seems to be hoping to go home soon.'

Greg nodded. 'I'm flying him back to Sealbank in the morning. Though what good he'll be with his leg in plaster . . .'

'But you'll be back before Friday,' Laura interrupted, brushing gently against him. 'You promised you'd be there!'

'I shall be there.' He patted her arm reassuringly, then glanced at Kate, but appeared to be in no mood for elaboration.

See if I care, she thought. But it wasn't easy to sip champagne and look nonchalant at the same time.

'Darling—Laura—I simply must see you . . .' A pink-haired dowager descended, then bore away her glittering prize, leaving Greg and Kate quite alone.

'Did McInnes give you a very bad time?' Greg asked, handing Kate's empty glass to a hovering waiter. He didn't take another one—perhaps he thought she had drunk enough already. Kate tried not to grin. Maybe he was right.

'Oh, Dougal and I just had a little chat,' she

shrugged, glancing down and flicking one of the shoe-string bows on her otherwise bare shoulders. And then, slowly, she began to remember the outcome of that conversation—and the decision she had made. Had she really? She stared up at Greg with wide, incredulous eyes, blinked a couple of times—then swallowed. But maybe he had changed his mind. Maybe he would rather just keep Laura. Her eyes narrowed. It was no good—she just didn't like Laura.

'I think you had better come and sit down.' A note of reproof and amusement in Greg's voice. 'Come on,' he took her arm, 'before you fall down. How much of that stuff have you had?'

'Only two glasses.'

'And you last ate . . .?'

'I had something at six o'clock.' But it took a surprising amount of concentration to manoeuvre her lips around that one.

Without further argument Greg steered her towards the conservatory. The white circular seat was still unoccupied and they sat down on the far side out of sight from the doorway, surrounded by an exotic paradise of foliage.

Greg crossed his legs and put a nonchalant arm on the seat behind her. Glossy, moth-eaten leaves hung above his head. They could have been in another world.

It was more difficult to start than she had imagined. How could you tell a man you had thought it over and had decided to become his mistress?

'Were you serious?' she began, glancing down at

her hands folded demurely in her lap, like someone out of a Jane Austen novel. But there all resemblance ended. 'I mean about what you said the other day,' she continued, 'about staying down here.'

His mouth hardened and his eyes veiled over. 'Quite serious. Why do you ask?'

'In—in spite of Laura?' Still Kate hedged and Greg looked puzzled. Then his brow cleared.

'As you said yourself, she's for the bright lights.'

Kate nodded. Yes. Somehow you couldn't imagine Laura bouncing around Sealbank in a mud-spattered truck. And after all, Greg spent a lot of time in town. He would probably continue seeing her as often as before.

She picked nervously at the silk folds across her knees. If only he wasn't quite so attractive—quite so exactly how she thought a man should be. Except for all his bad points, of course. But just at this moment she couldn't remember any.

'I—I was thinking—if the offer's still open ...' Was she doing this for Big John, for the company—or for herself? Everything started to fall to pieces inside her. This couldn't possibly be real.

'Oh, the offer's still open.' His voice was barely above a whisper, yet there was an edge of triumph in the quiet tone. No wonder. It probably wasn't every day his ideas came together quite so easily.

'I don't know why I made such a fuss before,' Kate nattered on, simply to break the silence. 'It isn't as if we're strangers ...'

'No!'

'No!'

Stalemate.

'So what happens now?' she asked eventually, glancing up at him again, and catching her breath. She hadn't been prepared for the curious intentness of his expression. But it gradually faded.

'What happens now?' he repeated, the corners of his mouth lifting fractionally. 'You mean now—this minute?' He raised his hand to her cheek and gently turned her face towards him. 'Nothing, Kate. Absolutely nothing.'

As he stared down at her time seemed to stand still. Water dripped off a plant, somewhere behind them. The warm, moist atmosphere enveloped her, enveloped them both, she supposed, and wrapped them up in a scented world of their own.

The soft silk gathers of her dress rose and fell. She had never been so physically aware of every inch of her body. She felt alive—trapped—deliriously happy —and frightened to death.

Was Greg reading her mind? For a second he seemed to be responding equally, wanting her as much as she wanted him. Then for some reason his eyes glistened with anger. 'So much for scruples,' he murmured, almost inaudibly. 'Yours or mine.' His quiet menace practically stopped Kate's heart.

After that there was just no escape. When they returned to the ballroom, Greg was beside her. She was led away and introduced to someone else, but over their shoulder she could see him still watching her.

Watching and waiting. Waiting for the reception to end? Waiting to return to the hotel? For Kate the rest of the evening spiralled into a haze. People came and went, she danced several times, but afterwards couldn't have said with whom or what music was played. Her mouth felt dry with tension, but she kept well away from the champagne. She was going to need a very clear head tonight to deal with whatever was coming her way.

And then Greg just disappeared. Kate realised for the past five minutes she hadn't seen him. Laura was absent as well. Was this to be her reprieve? Maybe she would have something for which to thank the Governor's daughter, after all.

Eventually Kate collected her wrap, keeping a wary eye out for the familiar chestnut head as she came downstairs. But there was no sign of him, although the hall was crowded. She spent an anxious few minutes waiting for the car, but at last it arrived, and she was in it, driving away from Government House and, heaven be praised, she was alone.

She sank back in the deep leather seat and sighed with relief. Never mind if Greg and Laura were together somewhere. Never mind if he hadn't really wanted her. She couldn't have coped with him anyway. He was far too dangerous, too experienced, all too, too much, altogether.

The car turned out of the driveway and purred quietly along the single-track road. The Residence was on one side of the town, the Bryants' hotel on the other; and she was thankful that the journey would give her time to unwind.

The luxurious interior of the ancient car helped as well. It was comforting, its mahogany trim and plushness reminding her of the elegance from another age. She let it envelop her, while her mind wandered back over the evening.

Greg obviously hadn't meant a word he had said. Perhaps the humiliation of offering herself to him was payment enough. Payment for her deception—not payment for the concession. There wouldn't be any chance of that now.

They drove around the harbour, deserted at this time of night. Then the car began to climb the hill and after a few moments it turned off the road and bumped gently along the track towards the headland. Kate could see one or two lights still shining from the hotel; there was a car turning round in front of the entrance and its headlights dazzled as it came towards them, far too fast, she thought, on such a narrow road.

Her driver seemed to think so too, and he muttered quietly to himself as the low, throaty sports car flashed past. But then he was pulling up in front of the entrance himself, getting out to assist her, and wishing her 'goodnight' as she hurried indoors.

The heavy oak door was difficult to fasten, and she turned round, making sure it was properly shut, before heading towards the reception desk. But fear froze her steps. Someone was there before her—a tall, dark figure leaning against the counter, ankles crossed, chin practically on his chest, as he sleepily contemplated the tiled floor. Then he slowly raised his eyes to meet hers, and there was a wealth of menace in the searching appraisal.

'I'm glad Laura brought me back just in time,' Greg said quietly, but the soft timbre of his voice was rich, vibrant and sensual. 'I believe we have some unfinished business to attend to,' he added, uncoiling himself slowly to his full, forbidding height. 'This is what you call the day of reckoning.' And when she looked appalled, he made things worse by adding, 'And you won't be able to talk your way out of this situation, I promise you.'

For an incredible moment Kate knew she didn't want to talk her way out of any situation Greg Henderson might devise. Apart from loving him for all the right reasons, there were all those other reasons; reasons he was displaying to such advantage right now. He was so physical, so superbly masculine and predatory, and her body responded to him even at this distance. She felt her limbs tremble with a wonderful, exhilarating dread, which gradually pulsated through her until it filled her mind and spirit totally. But common sense kept her eyes lowered so that he shouldn't see.

The hotel seemed deserted. Where had everyone gone? A treacherous silence echoed between them.

'I have no intention of talking my way out of any situation,' Kate declared, with a courage she was far

from feeling. 'There isn't one—a situation, I mean,'
and she marched towards the reception desk to collect her key.

'There's a situation, all right,' Greg continued,
stretching out and catching her arm as she tried to
push past him. 'And is this what you happen to be
looking for?' he asked, holding up a large key that
swung from a metal tag.

Instinct told Kate just which lock it would fit and
anger rose above every other emotion.

'And what gives you the right to take it?' she demanded, pretending she wasn't practically flattened
against his chest.

'You give me the right, Kate—remember?' and she
was pulled even closer as his lips parted in cruel delight.

'I never suggested . . .'

'Oh, yes, you did.'

She blinked, remembering, 'Well, I've—I've
changed my mind. The deal's off.'

'No way,' he interrupted, as she wriggled to get
free, but only the shawl escaped, and his eyes glistened at the expanse of creamy skin beneath. 'No one
walks out on me,' he said thickly, resting the end of
the cold metal key against her cheek. 'A deal is a
deal, down here, Kate.' And as his voice lowered to a
husky purr, he allowed the key to slide slowly down
her neck.

Kate strained away, but leaning backwards did nothing to alleviate Greg's delight. The key sank lower
and lower and her spine tingled as it caressed an icy

line between her breasts. She knew he felt her flinch and she saw the immediate response in his eyes as they gleamed satanically. Then tension angled his face and ran down the length of him. He was suddenly vitally alive and very dangerous.

Panic brought her to life first.

'Well, I say the deal's off,' she began quickly. 'And that's an end to it. You can hardly drag me screaming up the stairs.'

'Try me!' he suggested, the idea instantly appealing, and Kate cursed herself for making such a silly remark.

'This is all quite ridiculous.' Perhaps plain common sense would work. 'You've had your little game, Mr Henderson.' She tried not to shrink further away from him as she held out her hand. 'Now, if you'll just give me . . .'

'It'll be a pleasure . . .' he announced, sweeping her into his arms and sending her world crazy.

She stared around helplessly, thunderstruck, dumb with amazement. He couldn't really carry her up the stairs—okay, so he could. But supposing someone came out of a room, but no one did, and he didn't seem tired or puffed, or even to notice very much that he was carrying anything more than a feather-weight.

It was all so unexpected and nerve-racking that Kate was being deposited on her feet outside the bed-room door before she even had time to think about screaming.

Greg fitted the key and turned it. He switched on

the low light inside and motioned her to precede him, and, still in a daze, she complied.

Hearing the door close behind her, she turned, half hoping . . . But there was to be no reprieve. Greg stood with his back against the door. She heard the key click again, then he removed it and slipped it into his dark jacket pocket.

She was trapped by the lion as surely as if this was his den. For a second the world stood still, until he slowly came towards her.

'This is where civilisation stops, Kate,' he said evenly, and fear managed to put words into her mouth.

'Just because you've got me up here,' she blurted, 'it doesn't mean . . . I'm not giving up . . .'

'I'm counting on it. How very tame if you were.' He went to grab her, but she was too quick for him, and his eyes ignited with a mixture of challenge and delight. 'You don't think you can actually get away from me?' he asked, tapping his pocket lightly, and there was no need to say more.

She glared at him. 'I'll—I'll . . .'

'Scream?' he suggested. 'But we already know that you won't.' He came two paces nearer and she retreated behind the easy chair.

'Look, maybe I was rash—earlier—at the reception . . .'

'Oh, you were, honey, very rash. Do you often make such mistakes?' He stood in the middle of the room quite patiently, as if he knew he had only to make an effort and she would be his.

Kate could have cried with frustration. What a position to be in! She wanted him—how desperately she wanted him. But like this—as a payment—part of a business deal? Never! Why had she been crazy enough to have imagined otherwise? Could it have been the champagne? But how to get out of it now? Perhaps she could appeal to his better nature—if he had one. But that hadn't worked downstairs—would it work up here?

'Maybe we should call a truce,' she began carefully, risking all by coming out from behind her barricade. She knew her hair was tumbled in disarray, the pink, swirly dress made her look delicate, fragile, and instinct told her to shine wide, innocent eyes towards her captor. 'I think—perhaps—it's all been a big mistake,' she tried to soothe. 'I'm sure neither of us meant . . .'

'Like hell I did!' Greg retorted, crossing the space between them in a long stride. Firm, powerful hands grasped her arms, and he towered over her aggressively. 'I told you this was one situation you weren't going to talk your way out of,' he reminded her. 'You picked the wrong guy, Kate, when you started playing your games with me. Now I'm going to show you what happens to such impetuous young ladies. It'll be something to tell them, back in London.' He paused, and allowed his eyes to rove freely over her. 'Always supposing you make it back there in one piece,' he added ominously.

Kate fought and wriggled, as fiercely as when he had dragged her out of the truck. But this time he didn't change his mind. This time he only laughed before scooping the hair away from her ear and bending to kiss her neck.

His hand in her hair forced her head way back. He kissed her throat, then the other side of her neck, until his mouth finally found hers.

Now the onslaught really began. There was no love, no tenderness—just a ruthless mastery that sent life throbbing through her as savage hands explored her aching body.

She tried to resist, to murmur her protest, but it wasn't really a protest. It was a sharp cry of delight as his fingers found the soft warmth he desired. Somehow she had stopped struggling, her arms had found their way around his neck. He felt so good next to her. So vitally alive and exciting; and suddenly she forgot all her fears, all the complications. She loved him, wasn't that enough?

Practically before her decision was made, Greg became aware of the change. His mouth gentled, then he suddenly pulled back and wild, dark eyes rippled their question.

'Kate, you don't mean——? You haven't ...' he began breathlessly, and when she made a helpless little gesture of acquiescence, he gave a low, husky sigh. 'And we've been driving each other wild!' He was exasperated, overjoyed, furious and delighted, and Kate allowed herself to be kissed all over again.

Only this time when he drew her close, the firm pressure was total, the inevitableness of the outcome written in every lingering caress.

His fingers picked at a silken bow and the dress sagged as it came undone. He moved to the other shoulder, kissing away her protests, and as the second tie unfurled she clutched at the front to stop the dress from falling down.

'That sure is some fancy outfit,' Greg murmured, delighted at his handiwork; then he was scooping her into his arms again and depositing her tenderly on the bed.

'You rogue—you shouldn't . . .'

'Shouldn't I?' he murmured, gently smoothing aside a lock of her hair, then his eyes sparkled as they met her own.

Kate threw caution and reserve to the winds, and soon they were both tangled in frothy pink silk. Greg muttered goodnaturedly, held both her hands together on the pillow, and stilled her protests with magnetic eyes as he slowly eased the dress away.

If Kate had imagined all this happening to her some day, she had supposed there would be embarrassment, confusion, but there was neither. This was no tumble in the dark—no uncontrolled passion getting out of hand. The outcome was guaranteed, but there was no rush, and it was a joy for Greg to see her. To touch her body—to bend and kiss her tenderly.

But gradually his gentle caress became more positive and he was altering the joy and love she felt for him into sharp, biting pleasure. Surely now ... But still he waited, building her up and up, until she cried out with a mixture of despair and exhilaration.

But somehow Greg was keeping a fine edge on control. 'Hush,' he whispered, not to soothe or calm her, but so that he had the pleasure of driving her crazy all over again. But then he was suddenly still, his eyes questioning, tension showing on a face where passion had ruled a moment before.

'It isn't every day I get someone as delectable as you fly in,' he murmured, casting a shadow right over her as he came closer.

'I was a very special passenger,' she whispered, momentarily as pleased with herself as he appeared to be. Then darkness came crashing in as the full meaning of his words hit her. Why on earth had she allowed herself to forget? This was just a game for him. At best, snapping people's names off passenger lists; at worst, retribution for the opposition. And she was here with him, about to make love with him, a total commitment to add to her devotion. And what must he be thinking of her? Some little P.R. girl prepared to go to any lengths to secure the concession? Heavens, she had forgotten all about that ages ago.

Greg was moving closer, becoming more insistent, and panic rushed in. She couldn't—she just couldn't let him ... There had to be more to it than this. There just had to be!

'Kate, honey, what's the matter?' How quickly he noticed her change of mood again. 'It'll be all right,' he assured. 'Trust me.' And then he seemed to realise it wasn't just nerves.

She blinked, and suddenly the world turned upside down.

'Aren't you forgetting something?' she murmured, through gathering sadness and confusion.

'Forgetting?' Greg was gently nibbling her ear. Now he paused and looked down at her inquisitively.

'Don't we have some unfinished business to attend to first?' she explained, saying the worst thing she could think of. 'A deal is a deal, you said.' Her voice lost its power and she trailed into silence.

Greg's face underwent a slow, tormenting change. 'Business before pleasure, you mean?' His lips curled and he looked suddenly ruthless. 'But this is the Southern Hemisphere, Kate. Down here we say pleasure before business.' His eyes were dark with anger and disgust. 'But you don't think there's really going to be any deal, do you? That I'd give away one bucketful of my land?' he managed to ask, between tight lips. Then he slowly took in every trembling detail lying beneath him, before adding with terrible finality, 'And I certainly wouldn't let some little tramp like you wheedle it out of me!'

CHAPTER ELEVEN

KATE sat in the Land Rover between the two men as it trundled along the deserted road towards the airport.

Behind the steering wheel, Dougal McInnes sat as gruff and silent as she would have expected. Since her phoning him early that morning and arranging a time to be collected, he had hardly spoken two words to her.

The engineer sat on Kate's other side. He was equally silent, but understandably lost in a world of his own, and she guessed he was already thinking about the problems he would have to contend with on the mainland.

But silence suited her just fine. It wasn't a good day. It was a sad, dismal, quite dreadful day. The sooner she could leave Drake Island, with all its tormenting memories, the sooner she would be able to restore her peace of mind. Or would she?

Could you ever get over someone like Greg Henderson? Having loved him, how would anyone else compare? Even the fact that he hated her was quite under-

standable, and part of her was pleased that he
wouldn't give up his land. What had he said once—
'Not at any price'. 'Not even to save your head'. Kate
blinked through the windscreen and saw the airport
buildings in the distance. But what about saving my
heart? she wondered. No. His land would come before everything. Because it had to last longer, she supposed. In trust, for ever. Hadn't he said something
like that, as well?

She tried not to remember that terrible scene in
her room last night. But the image wouldn't fade.
Greg's loathing for her wouldn't be dispelled by a
few hours' restless sleep. And the excitement she had
felt for him couldn't be dispelled either, and together
both emotions strung on her nerves until she wanted
to scream.

The little white jet with its long, spiteful nose was
already waiting on the tarmac as they staggered into
the reception hall with their gear.

'Right waste of time all this is,' Dougal muttered,
casting an eye towards several men struggling to erect
some sort of banner.

Kate glanced around; there was certainly something going on. Far more people about than when she
had flown in last week.

'What's it all for?' she asked, as their cases were
weighed and labelled.

'The Governor's fond farewell,' he said, as if she
was crazy not to realise. 'You went to the reception
last night—didn't you read the invitation? He's off

to pastures new, and tomorrow he moves out—lock
stock and barrel. It would appear, to the sound o
trumpets,' he added with asperity, as the local band
could be seen gathering outside for a practice.

Lock, stock and barrel? Did that include Laura? I
a daze Kate handed Dougal her passport and visa and
he disappeared to make all the arrangements for he
unscheduled trip.

If Laura was moving out—and Greg wouldn't be
seeing her . . . For a moment hope spun crazily, bu
there was no sense in it. It didn't change anything. I
was just a false alarm.

She sighed, and gazed round hopelessly. It was al
so familiar. The same lounge, the same door with it
frosted glass through which Greg had appeared, and
the whole affair had begun. Only then there had been
adventure and hope in the air—whereas now . . .

Kate refused to dwell further on the difference be
tween this visit and her first. At any moment she ex
pected Greg to materialise, but there was no sign o:
him, so she hid in a corner and tried to make con
versation with her fellow passenger.

Gradually everything settled to quietness, she
stopped trying to talk, the engineer lit a cigarette, and
she stared out of the window, watching a tanker draw
up alongside the jet and begin refuelling. The sound
of a typewriter stopped. A telephone rang and was
quickly picked up. Silence. An ominous silence, and
Kate began to wriggle her toes uncomfortably. Where
was Dougal? Why was he taking so long? The tanker

had driven away. Where was the pilot?

The clock on the cream-painted wall jerked its noisy way between seconds. She stared at it in fascination. Shouldn't they be boarding by now? Why hadn't someone brought back her passport? She glanced across at the engineer, who turned the pages of a report and simultaneously flicked ash into a pedestal bin provided for the purpose. He didn't look on edge, yet he didn't know about Greg Henderson. Had Greg really flown back to Sealbank with Tom? Or was he lurking nearby—waiting to pounce?

Everything would be all right if she could just go —now. Without seeing him again. Last night's pain was still too sharp; but, as if her dread had conjured it up, there was a sudden, unmistakable sound of a door viciously banging—it was a wonder the glass didn't break. Just as she had thought before. And once more she felt an odd sensation in her knees as adversity stormed to meet her.

'In my office—now.' Greg the sheep-farmer—Greg the protector of wild-life—Greg the dominant lover— stood before her, in a towering rage.

This wasn't the moment to weaken. Her companion looked about to retort. Heavens, there was no time for *that* scene!

'If you've anything to say,' she began, managing to stand up and so reducing her disadvantage by a few feet, 'then you can say it here.'

'Not on your life!' Greg grabbed her arm and froze the engineer in his tracks with one look. 'You'll be travelling alone,' he roared at the startled man. 'See McInnes if you want an explanation. *I* haven't got the time.' And then he tried to manoeuvre Kate towards the office, but she wasn't having any of that.

'Take your hands off me! No—it's all right,' she added hastily, seeing the engineer leap to her defence again. Maybe it would be best to go into Greg's office. If they stayed here things could get tough. 'But I will be coming with you,' she said over her shoulder, managing to break free from Greg's hold at the same time.

'Like hell you will,' he muttered ominously. 'Nobody runs out on me.'

'You can't stop me,' she flung at him.

'Can't I?' There was a menacing grin on his face which remained until they reached his office immediately beneath the control tower.

He marched across to the desk and picked up the phone, leaving Kate to stare around, bewildered, as she adjusted the many facets of the man to include this new image. Papers, meteorological charts, notices to pilots, all pinned on pegboard, and the whole vista below of two runways with their system of 'stop' and 'go' lights, as complicated, she guessed, as any major traffic system.

It was all fascinating; she was momentarily silenced, until the sound of Greg's voice brought her back to reality.

'. . . and he can leave when he likes,' he was saying. 'It's been sorted out. There'll only be one passenger.'

'No, there won't.' Kate rushed to the phone, but he slammed down the receiver, his dark eyes glinting with triumph. Damn the man! How dare he? The dread she had felt at seeing him again was instantly replaced by anger. 'You've no right to hold me here ...' she broke off, seeing her passport on his blotter.

'I've every right.' He followed her gaze to the desk. 'Your visa's out of date. If you'd landed in South America you might have found yourself in jail.'

'Don't be ridiculous, you're exaggerating, and anyway,' Kate tossed her head and made a grab for the documents, 'it can't be out of date,' she added, flicking open the dark blue cover to check. 'See?' she said gleefully, then suddenly realising this was the vital paperwork, she made a dash for the door.

He was there before her, catching her wrist and taking the passport without effort.

'Fancy that, now. How unfortunate. Especially as I'll discover *that* half an hour after your plane has gone.'

It was useless trying to rush the door again. Kate stuck her hands in her jacket pocket and stormed across the deep carpet.

'I said no one runs out on me, Kate, and I meant it.' She swung round and glared at him as he perched on the edge of his desk. 'Did you really think you could get off so lightly?'

'You're the one who ran out, as I remember,' she countered, turning to face him squarely. 'I was perfectly willing ...' She gave an embarrassed little cough and faded out.

'You sure were—perfectly.' He paused, emphasising his meaning, then added. 'But what changed your mind? Why did you suddenly wave the concession in my face?'

'A deal is a deal,' Kate hedged. 'But you hadn't meant it, had you?' She tried to defend herself by attacking. Anything to get away from the real reason she had been willing—or had suddenly changed her mind. 'Not one bucketful, you said,' she reminded him forcefully.

'And I meant that, as well.' She could tell he did—it showed in his eyes.

'And you've always meant it, haven't you?' she flung at him, finally seeing the truth of it all. His one letter to London—all Dougal's reports. Emphatic, dominant refusal, right from the beginning. Whose bright idea had it been to send her down here to try and persuade him otherwise?

'I never had any intention of signing any kind of deal with your company, now or in the future.' He actually seemed surprised that she should think differently.

'Then why ...?' she broke off, pacing uncertainly towards the window and staring out. If he had never intended signing, then why had he suggested she stay at Sealbank? 'What was the point?' she tried again, not even sure if she had spoken the words out loud.

'Isn't that obvious?' Greg answered, proving she

had spoken and that he understood her train of thought. 'Don't you really know, even now, Kate?'

She turned towards him again, her face a mirror of confusion, as much because of the gentleness in his voice as for the words he was using.

'I wanted you to stay—simply for that reason,' he went on, looking perplexed. 'After last night I thought that would have been perfectly obvious.'

Yes, it had been obvious, thought Kate. He had needed her physically—as a demanding, dominant lover. But surely that should only be part of a relationship? All the rest was important too.

And was there really any other feeling on his part? She tried to think of all the times he had spoken to her —and she suddenly had a clear image of him behind his desk at Sealbank. She tried to remember the words he had used then, the way he had fiddled with a pencil, rolling it along the mahogany top ... And then she saw it—the photograph. Of course. That was why he had asked her to stay. Laura was leaving. There weren't that many women on Drake, and she guessed Greg Henderson was the kind of man who would need the comfort of a woman. No, she couldn't compete with Laura, and he hadn't chosen between them. He had just been making sure of the available goods until the next batch of passengers flew in, as he had admitted himself, last night—as she had really known herself, all along. Sadness engulfed her.

'Last night doesn't make any difference to anything,' she began, finding the words from somewhere.

She spread her hands in a useless little gesture. 'I still have a job to do—elsewhere. Life doesn't stop because one project failed.'

'Life wouldn't stop if you stayed here,' he said carefully. But his head was bent lower now, towards his chest, and he was looking at her through a veil of thick lashes.

'Perhaps not—for a while,' and when he contrived to look puzzled, something just blew in Kate's mind. 'Look, I'm not an absolute moron—I do realise,' she blurted. 'There's no need denying it. I've just found out. Laura's leaving.' And when he still didn't comment, she practically shouted, 'So you'll miss her, won't you?'

'A lot of people will miss her,' he said quietly, and there was an odd light behind the shadow in his eyes.

'What I mean is—she won't be available . . .' but his altering expression rendered her silent.

He simply began to smile. Slowly at first, from the corners of his mouth, then his cheeks lifted and joy radiated from his eyes.

She had never seen him—anyone—smile so completely. It stopped thought, words, even existence, for the time its magic remained on his face.

The sound of a plane warming up outside gradually penetrated, and Kate tried to blink herself back to reality. Oh, she was going to miss this man dreadfully. He was so alive, so much a part of life. He had become so much a part of her life that the thought of being without him was appalling.

'And you think I'd try to keep you down here just because Laura's leaving?' The smile had gone and he ran distraught fingers through his hair, heaving himself off the desk as he did so.

Kate backed away.

'I've—I've read the statistics,' she stammered, because it did all sound rather foolish when she put it into words. 'And I know there aren't that many women ...'

'No,' Greg moaned, with a long, agonising sigh. 'Not that many. Not if you happen to be half a dozen Turkish sultans with amazing appetites,' he exploded, scraping the depths of his imagination. 'But I do have the pick of every available woman on this island, which is quite enough variety for me. And I've been told the new Governor has three very attractive daughters.' He broke off, coming slowly towards her, and this time she allowed herself to be captured. His hand on her arm was gentle, and he carefully wound a strand of hair behind her ear before continuing. 'If you don't stay, who'll come rescuing shepherds?—or cook my dinner?' he asked, his voice husky with emotion, as he ran firm, strong hands down her back. 'Or who'll warm my bed?' he whispered into her ear.

Kate dissolved. Greg Henderson was a very persuasive man. A few months doing everything he suggested was a tantalising prospect.

'But there's still a problem, isn't there, Kate?' and she looked up at him with wide, surprised eyes. 'This love idea you've got,' he went on cautiously. 'The reason you still haven't said you'll stay.'

Kate moved uncomfortably in his arms. No, she couldn't stay without his love. But how to tell him? How to escape from this situation before she simply shattered.

Outside the noise became suddenly deafening. They both turned towards the window as Inpet's charter flight took off for South America. She wriggled out of Greg's arms and put a hand to her face in confusion. He was watching every move she made with quiet deliberation.

'So I have to stay on for a couple of extra days,' she began hopelessly, indicating the empty sky. 'But it doesn't alter things—I still have my scruples, as you call them.'

'I'm sure McInnes put the idea into your head,' Greg began slowly, and somewhat vaguely, 'but are you suggesting that you even contemplated climbing into my bed without loving me?'

Kate could have faded away with embarrassment. How could he? Did he enjoy seeing her so near despair?

'I'd had quite a bit of champagne,' she defended.

His eyes flickered, but he wasn't convinced. 'It might have given you the courage to say the words— but not to give you the idea in the first place. And it had worn off, anyway, by the time you got back to the hotel.'

Kate stared at him in confusion. Did he really know everything about her?

'I had a woman in my arms last night, Kate.' His voice was mellow. 'A warm, loving very lovely lady. But she didn't stay long—she disappeared, just like Cinderella—only it was way past midnight.' Kate automatically acknowledged his banter with a brief smile. 'But she was real, Kate, wasn't she? I didn't imagine her?'

The real me—the inside me? Kate wanted to ask. So he had seen straight through her. What did it mean? A new and different emotion clambered its way among all the rest that bubbled inside her.

'And after she'd gone,' Greg continued, when she still didn't speak. 'I was left with a bright, career girl offering deals that didn't interest me at all. Was I wrong, Kate, to see that other girl? The one who I thought loved me?'

Kate blinked away tears and strolled back towards the desk, running her finger along the wooden trim.

The more he spoke the worse everything became. Why had he trapped her in this corner? She either had to admit to loving him—or something far worse. When she eventually left this island, what memories would she leave behind with him? Those of a foolish girl who had fallen in love, or a ruthless woman prepared to go to any lengths for her Company?

Greg was waiting for her answer, standing with his back to the window, a dark silhouette against the brightness. But he wasn't just looking and waiting with his eyes. There was an abyss of unspoken words and thoughts lying between them; hope and confusion all tangled together. The atmosphere in the room was almost tangible, and she realised she would be leaving much of herself on Drake. Surely it was only possible to leave behind the truth.

'She was real,' she began in a tremulous whisper, 'that other person you saw. But she's the one with the hang-up, you see.' She glanced uncertainly over her shoulder towards him.

'The one that worries about love,' Greg prompted, and Kate nodded. Silence remained for a few moments until he added quietly, 'and does she love me?'

Kate swallowed, gazed down at the carpet, and nodded again. She couldn't look at his face, but what point would there be if she had?

'And did you think Laura was a very special lady to me?'

'Yes,' she murmured, down at the carpet.

'And were you in a dreadful turmoil sorting out McInnes and your job—and loving me?'

'Yes.' Again, what else was there to say?

Amusement touched his voice. 'But didn't you realise that I've loved you for a very long time?'

'Yes ...' she began automatically. Then she stopped, slowly gazed up at him, and opened wide, astounded eyes. 'But you hardly know me,' were the only ridiculous words that sprang to her lips.

He didn't seem to mind. 'But I've dreamt of you coming for a very long time,' he admitted, moving slowly towards her. 'It's very handy having access to passenger lists,' he began quickly, taking her into his arms and stopping her retort with a quick kiss. 'And when this crazy photographer waltzed in, flashing her eyes and leaving gadget-bags all over the place, I guess you could say I knew a very, very special lady had flown in.'

This was getting all too much for Kate, so she remained silent.

'And that's when everything started going wrong,' he went on. 'One minute you were this lovely, delectable lady,' he emphasised his appreciation with a slow, exploratory caress, 'and the next minute you were one of the McInnes team. I was confused, Kate —practically out of my mind half the time.'

'And at Sealbank,' she began carefully, because everything was going crazy and she had to concentrate like mad. 'And at Sealbank,' she repeated, 'when you asked me to stay—you loved me then?' Such a readjustment of all her ideas was very nearly as overpowering as her need to dissolve into him.

Greg passed a hand over his face, as if he was trying to erase a terrible dream. 'Don't remind me,' he muttered. 'Talk about making a hash of everything!' He smiled down and smoothed her cheek affectionately. 'But you had me flying upside down, Kate, with nothing on the clock but the maker's name. And that's low—pretty low.' He paused and smiled brightly. 'And I'm usually so—together—when I deal with my ladies.'

Kate remembered how slick he had always seemed with Laura. It was rather lovely to think that he couldn't play that particular game with herself.

'And I couldn't believe that you would really want to stay down here—in such backwoods country . . .'

She blushed, remembering all her earlier comments. 'I didn't really mean . . .'

'I know. But Drake Island will be a lot different, love, from the kind of thing you've been used to,' he said, gently stroking her hand. 'That is,' he hesitated, 'if you do want to stay.'

If she wanted to! Kate glowed inside. He loved her. He wanted her to stay. It wouldn't matter where, didn't he realise that?

'I think I rather would like to stay,' she smiled up at him. 'And I realise it will all be quite different and I'll have to get used to things. But it's nearer than the moon,' she explained, 'and much nicer than Outer Mongolia.' He frowned, bemused, but before he could comment, she cried, 'But what on earth can I say to Dougal?'

'Nothing,' came Greg's immediate response. '*I* shall have great pleasure in explaining it all. But we do have this other problem.' Now she frowned, and he prolonged the agony of doubt with a drawn-out silence. 'On Drake,' he began eventually, 'love isn't enough. There aren't that many women about, you see. And when a man finds one—and intends keeping her—well then . . .' he perched back on the edge of the desk and folded Kate tightly between his legs, 'he makes an honest woman of her. All the ring on her finger bit. The signed and sealed agreement. *Our* variety,' he added hastily. 'What do you say, Kate, mmm?'

'Yes, please,' she whispered, hoping he wouldn't say one more unbelievable, magical word. If he did she would simply burst with pleasure.

It took Greg a minute to wash away every doubt and fear of the past few days. And a further minute to freshen last night's wild excitement.

'Greg, no, please, not here . . .' But he only laughed, bit her neck playfully, then eased her away from him.

She watched in fascination as he strolled nonchalantly round the desk, bending towards the intercom and flicking a switch.

'I am not to be disturbed,' he instructed, his eyes shining at Kate with magnificent audacity. 'Not under *any* circumstances,' he added severely, and she guessed if Concorde should request an emergency landing, no one would dare to tell him.